PRAISE FOR SUSAN ISRAEL'S FIRST NOVEL, *OVER MY LIVE BODY*:

"Smart, witty, and delightfully unpredictable, Susan Israel's *Over My Live Body* is a truly wonderful debut. Highly recommended."
– Doug Corleone, author of *Good as Gone*

"A well written, delightful, interesting and fun read. Looking forward to book two!"
– Hotchpotch

"A smart, savvy mystery with a very likeable heroine and a twisted and labyrinth plot."
– Cayocosta72

"Page turning goodness with a tinge of suspense and a twist of shock."
– Cassandra M's Place

"A definite page-turner for me. It kept my interest and attention to the very end and I will be looking forward to the second book in the series."
– The Butler Did It

"Susan Israel has created an offbeat heroine, a strong woman intent on her career and determined to make it on her own regardless of what it takes to do so...recommended for mystery lovers."
– Booksie's Blog

STUDENT BODIES

STUDENT BODIES

SUSAN ISRAEL

Studio Digital CT, LLC
P.O. Box 4331
Stamford, CT 06907

Copyright © 2016 by Susan Israel
Jacket design by Barbara Aronica-Buck

Story Plant Paperback ISBN-13: 978-1-61188-227-8
Fiction Studio Books E-book ISBN-13: 978-1-943486-85-4

Visit our website at www.TheStoryPlant.com

First Story Plant paperback printing: May 2016
Printed in the United States of America

0 9 8 7 6 5 4 3 2 1

1

"You want to know what the problem is with these goils? They want it and they can't get it any other way, so they wear their blouses down to here so their tits are hanging out and wear their skirts up to their ass, and then they scream 'rape.'"

"You want to know what your problem is? You're a sexist pig!" I bellow at the radio. Dr. Joni tells the guy virtually the same thing and hangs up on him. The next caller wants to know how to protect herself. Everybody on radio talk shows is talking sexual assault these days in response to the ABC rapist, so named because his first victims virtually lived on the streets of Alphabet City. He didn't have to bang down doors to get to them and nobody paid much attention until he did start breaking in past a few doors, entering through a few open windows, and moving west to First, then Second Avenue. "I live on Third Avenue," the caller says, her voice shaky. "I'm a student at Tisch. I come home late at night. The security in my building is lousy. I think I've even been followed a couple of times."

I turn off the radio and look out of my own window. Force of habit. I know what it's like to be followed; I was stalked and abducted by a madman the end of last year and I still freeze when I hear footsteps come too close behind me. I still duck into stores where I have no intention of buying anything and wait until the coast is clear.

On the streets of New York City, the coast is never clear. There's always somebody likely to walk behind you, but they're not all out to *get* you. It's easier to believe this in the relative safety of my own apartment, behind a door with four locks, than when I'm out there though.

I live in a sublet on Waverly Place in the West Village, far enough from striking distance of the ABC rapist to feel safe from him. My past experience taught me valuable life lessons about protecting myself from harm. So did the counseling sessions to deal with post-traumatic stress. So did the detective who worked the case. I'm still dealing with him and not professionally anymore, though he never exactly stops acting like a cop when he's with me, which isn't as much as I'd like him to be. His name is Patrick Quick, Detective Second Grade, recently transferred from the First Precinct to the Ninth, which encompasses more turf and more work. I sometimes get to see him on his swing, which is what cops call their days off. I still think of it in kid terms as a seat suspended from a tree and sometimes feel like he's keeping me dangling on one, leaving me to propel myself back and forth until he figures out what he wants to do with me. *Quick indeed.*

He has the magical ability to pick up on brain waves though. He senses when I'm thinking about him just as he recognizes when a suspect is lying to him. The minute my iPhone rings, I know it's him. Hat Trick is the silly nickname I've heard his colleagues call him at the cop shop. There must be something to it. He's the David Copperfield of the NYPD, pulling clues out of thin air or pulling emotions out of wounded women like me. I hastily reach to turn off the radio when I hear his voice and realize I already did.

"Have you been listening to the radio?" he asks.

"No," I say. "Should I be?" My counselor strongly advised me not to listen to the all-news stations any more.

I used to depend on them to put me to sleep the way some people use white noise machines, and some of the reports I heard led me to associate other crimes with what I was going through. After it was over, every crime story I heard gave me nightmares. Quick put his foot down too. No more WCBS, no more 1010 WINS. No newspapers either. Talk radio sometimes serves the general purpose that the former did. Until today.

"You know you shouldn't be." He pauses. "I got a call from Rubenstein over in the Sixth. There was an assault on Jane Street last night. The vic lived on East Seventh. She was on her way home from visiting a friend when it happened."

Neither Rubenstein nor Quick deal with sex crimes directly; there are detectives specifically trained to deal with that. They only get involved when the crime goes beyond rape. His use of the past tense isn't lost on me. "Did ABC do it?" Up to now, ABC hasn't killed any of his victims.

"We're looking into it. Right now it doesn't fit his MO," he says. "Not even close. But it's not too far from where you are. I just want you to be aware of what's going on." He clears his throat. "So you'll be careful."

"I've never stopped being careful." I assure him, switching the phone from one sweaty hand to the other. His concern evokes other physical responses in me too. *I could use a little more of that hyper-vigilance right here in this apartment, right now, Detective Quick, sir.* He's doing a week of day tour, though, 8:00 a.m. to 4:15 p.m., so immediate police protection is out of the question, but I decide to feel him out with a Mae West line. "How about this afternoon when you get off work, you come by and check my locks?"

"Can't tonight, Delilah, I'm sorry," he says. "I have to stop by Alison's."

Alison is his sister, recently released from drug rehab for the second time since December and he's told me that he suspects she's headed back for a longer stay; this is all he's told me about her. Alison is my sole competitor for his attention. I try not to resent it—she's sick—but I wonder if there's a family dynamic I don't know about that's retarding her recovery. I haven't dared to ask more about her than, "How is she doing?"

"I'll call you tonight after I've seen her," Quick promises. "Keep that door locked. Maybe I'll oil that deadbolt for you over the weekend."

Fine. That's the only thing in this apartment that *needs* lubrication right now. My phone slips out of my hand and rings in protest. *Damn.* I wipe my palms on my coverall. Quick is gone by the time I pick up the phone. I hit disconnect. The minute I do, it rings again. I wipe my palms again before answering.

But it's not Quick this time. "Delilah," a female voice whispers and then breaks into strangled sobs. "It's Sachi. Can you talk?"

The question shouldn't be can I, but will I. Sachi has always been known to blow me off in my moments of greatest need, but when she needed a shoulder to cry on, she's never hesitated to call. Except it's been months since she's dared to call and this time she really is crying. "What's wrong?"

"Can you come over?" she whimpers.

"Now?" Stupid question. I realize she must mean now or she wouldn't ask. It's just a delaying tactic. Her apartment is the last place I want to be. Also the last place she'd have wanted me to be in recent months, when she was so tight with her live-in lover that I thought only surgery could separate them. "What's going on, Sachi?"

"I was raped."

"What? When?" Later we'll get around to who, where and how.

"Last night. Late last night. What time is it?"

I look at the red LED display on my alarm clock. "Nine-fifty."

"I got home around five. Maybe after. It was starting to get light." She clears her throat. "Well, are you coming over or aren't you? I don't want to talk about this on the phone."

"I'll be there," I promise, trying not to think of all the calls she didn't return last December when I was in trouble, when I thought I needed her. "Have you reported it? Have you been to the hospital?"

All I get for an answer is silence and a 'call ended' alert.

2

The newspapers are full of it. LAST DANCE blares the headline of the *Post*. The victim Quick told me about was a principal dancer with the City Ballet, sidelined by an injured Achilles tendon, which made it all the more difficult for her to get away from the man who savagely attacked her last night, leaving her for dead in the gutter. Was it the same man who attacked all those other women in the East Village? *Was it the same man who attacked Sachi?*

The door to the stairwell leading up to Sachi's Prince Street apartment is propped open with a cinder block when I get there. I kick it aside with my foot so the door will lock after me and climb the stairs to the second floor, then stop to compose myself before climbing the next flight. I haven't seen or spoken to Sachi in months. I don't even know what I'm doing here. When my friend Morgan was in trouble, I rushed to be by his side. Something Sachi refused to do for me. She'd be better off calling the crisis hotline. Still here I am, in body if not entirely in spirit. I'm a sucker.

The door to Sachi's apartment is open too. She might as well put out a welcome mat: Come one, come all. The apartment looks like a set designer's idea of a crime scene; end tables upended, an arm torn from a brocade chair, broken dishes on the floor. I rap on the jamb. "Sachi?" A terrifying thought possesses me and I step back a few feet. *What if the rapist came back for seconds? What if he's inside now?* "Satch?" I holler, my voice loud enough in its panic to alert other neighbors of a potentially precarious situation.

Sachi struts out of the bathroom wearing a simple black slip dress, her head wrapped in a towel. "Were you here long? Sorry. I just got out of the shower."

"And you left the door open?"

"Every part of me was ripped open," she says briskly, like she's talking about an envelope. "What more can he do?"

"A lot more." I shake my head at her. "You've been to the hospital already then..."

"Uh, no." She rubs her scalp with the terry towel, avoiding my stare. "I didn't report it yet."

"Sachi, you're not supposed to shower or be washing your hair or anything like that; you just washed a whole lot of evidence down the drain." I don't have to be involved with a cop to know that basic fact of life.

She lifts a corner of the towel and peers at me. "I want you to go with me," she says in a tremulous baby voice. "I didn't want to go alone to tell some cop what was done to me." She wrinkles her nose at the word cop as much as at the recollection of what was done to her.

"What was done to you?" I know this has to be asked eventually and as much as I'm not sure I want to hear it, I know Sachi's going to have to tell it again and again and again. She might as well start with me.

"Oh..." she blows her nose into the towel and drops it on the floor. "You name it."

I look around the room again. "Here?"

"No," she shakes her head. "Not here. Right down the street. You know where there's this Italian bakery with an open stairwell...he grabbed my ankle and pulled me down the stairs and did it to me there."

"What happened here?"

"I did that." She kicks aside a shard of glass and slides her feet into Birkenstocks that she had evidently kicked across the room in her rage.

"Where's...uh...your boyfriend?" I can't remember if she ever even told me his name.

"Tom? Your guess is as good as mine."

Problems in paradise. No wonder she called me. I never met the mystery man she dumped her friends for, so I couldn't even begin to guess where he is now that he dumped her, if that's indeed the case. "Satch, I'm going to call the police. Where's the phone?"

She grabs my wrist. "Can't it wait till we get to the hospital? I just want to make sure he didn't give me a disease." She wrinkles her nose again. I can't believe this is all she's worried about. Like all they have to do is shoot her up with antibiotics, as a prophylactic, and everything will be fine—really, she can make like nothing ever happened to her.

"The hospital's going to notify the police anyway, Satch. It's up to you whether you file a complaint or not, but they're going to want to talk to you. There's a serial rapist and he killed someone last night." Not exactly the whole truth, since Quick told me that ABC wasn't being considered a suspect for that, but Sachi needs to come clean. She's coming to the hospital too clean, actually. I wonder how much evidence that shower destroyed. "I'll stay with you if they let me and I think they will. But in the meantime, I still think we should call the police before we go, so they can go over to the crime scene." I pick up the phone and automatically press the numbers for Quick's extension.

"They probably won't find anything there. I told you, he just did it to me on the stairs..."

A woman answers the phone. "Everybody's out of the office right now," she says when I ask for Quick. "If this is an emergency, I can page him or have someone else help you."

"I want to report a rape," I say. Sachi flinches.

"Address?" I tell her. "Where on Prince Street?" I tell her. "You want the First Precinct," she tells me. I'm not so sure about that. I remember some of the other detectives Quick worked with at the First before he was transferred and I want to talk to him before Sachi has to talk to them. "Could you page Detective Quick and tell him Delilah called and that I'm going to be over at the hospital with the victim and I'll call him from there?"

"I don't know when he'll be back."

"Ask him to call me at the hospital in about an hour."

"Which hospital did you say you're bringing her to?"

I cup my hand over the mouthpiece and hiss at Sachi. "You're not worried about getting pregnant from this, are you?"

She shakes her head. "I'm on the pill."

"Beth Israel," I say. "Tell him to call the emergency room there. Tell him it's not me—that he doesn't have to worry—just to call me there as soon as he can. Please."

"Who's that you called?" Sachi gives me the once over, like she's suddenly acknowledging there's a lot she doesn't know about what's been going on in my life. Even in a state of shock, Sachi has to be in the know.

"Detective friend of mine. He wasn't there. He'll call me at the hospital. Let's get going."

"I don't want to talk to any males about this."

"I'll talk to him, Satch. They have female detectives to handle this sort of thing, I'm sure." I wait for Sachi to lock the door. The tumbler clicks without a hitch. I would have dropped my keys five times by now if not more, had this happened to me. "Want to show me where it happened? So I can tell the police where to look, at least?"

She points down the street to a bilious green wrought-iron rail. "Down there."

I walk down the block and look down the stairwell, then back at Sachi, who looks bilious herself. "Pretty close to home. Did he take anything from you?"

"Aside from the obvious?"

"You know. Money. ID stuff, *any*thing with your name and address..."

"He was only interested in one thing and he took it. Can we *go* now, please?"

I shepherd her away from the scene of the crime and toward Sixth Avenue. "Come on, it's not that far," I coo. I can't say, "It's not going to be that bad." I don't know how bad it's going to be. An M5 bus hisses to a stop past Houston and I gently shove Sachi up the stairs ahead of me. Her fingers fidget in her purse. "I can't find my MetroCard..."

I dig into my fanny pack for all the change I can scoop and drop coins on the floor and into the box all the way to First Avenue.

3

"Wait a minute," the triage nurse tells us when we report to the emergency room window and whisper to her what happened. She gives Sachi the once over, taking in the expensive slip dress, the minimally made up doll face. No visible bruises on her, no imminent danger of her keeling over in front of the Jesus statue mounted on the wall, so she can wait and wait and wait. There are others in the waiting room that look worse off. Sachi looks like party material. An orderly smoking a cigarette on the outside loading dock leers in at us.

"I wish he'd go away," Sachi moans, repositioning herself, crossing her legs, showing more thigh. I stand up to try to block his view, uncomfortable that at the same time I'm making myself the focal point of his attention.

"How much longer is it going to be?" I ask the nurse at the desk.

"Just a few minutes. We're getting a room ready," she announces just as the automatic door leading to the ambulance loading dock parts. A couple of uniforms strut through. When they pass the second door, I recognize one of them as Officer Vinson, who has responded to my distress calls in the past. His old partner isn't with him. In his place is a female officer, a pony-tailed redhead who sizes both of us up with clear green eyes, trying to determine

17

who's the vic here. Vinson does a double take when he sees me and shakes his head.

"Someone over at the Ninth relayed a ten twenty-four, said to report here," he informs the triage nurse.

"It *wasn't me*," I whisper.

A bell signals the door to the ER open and the triage nurse waves us in and ushers us into a cubicle that smells very eau de Betadine. Officer Vinson follows us and falls in step with Sachi. "This is Officer O'Hara," he tilts his head toward his partner. "*We* call her Scarlett. You can call her Mary Louise. She's gonna ask you a few questions about what happened before the doc does what he's gotta do..."

"I want a *female* doctor," Sachi insists.

"Okay, I'm sure that can be arranged," Mary Louise assures her as the nurse continues to prep the room for the exam.

Vinson turns to me. "C'mon, I want to talk to you out in the hall." He holds the door open for me, his eyes riveted on Sachi who hasn't once met his stare head-on. I follow him into a small room across the hall. A couple of nurses look up from their double-acrostics and smile beguilingly at him, ignoring me completely. "Coffee on the burner if you want it," one says, like she's offering him a piece of her soul.

"And it's not even burned," says the other. Double enticement.

"Thanks, ladies. I've got some business to discuss here with a witness. Could I borrow the room for a few minutes?"

They're not going to get anywhere with him if they say no. "Later," he promises to one or both of them as they leave. The last one out the door turns around and winks.

"Want some coffee?" he asks, taking over the turf like he's the chairman of the board. I shake my head. He takes a sip, puts his Styrofoam cup on the counter and whips a notepad out of his pants pocket. "What can you tell me about this?"

"She didn't tell me much."

"What did she tell you?"

I lick my lips. "That she got raped." I'm not the victim and it's still difficult to talk about. "Someone grabbed her on the street—on Prince Street near Thompson—and pulled her down a stairwell there and raped her."

"She didn't report it until now?"

"She was in a state of shock, I guess."

"She a neighbor of yours or..."

"Friend." That seems to be pushing it. *A friend in need.* "She called me and that's all she told me, that she was raped. When I went over to her place, the apartment had been trashed, but she told me it happened outside and showed me where."

"So who trashed the apartment?"

"She said she did."

"You don't believe her?"

I don't believe anything about this morning so far. "When I first saw her apartment, I had the feeling it happened there."

"We'll be taking a look at it. She say anything about who did this to her...?"

"No."

"Or what he did?"

"She said, 'You name it.' "

"She got a boyfriend, Miss Price?"

"She did, last I knew."

"Where's he? Does he know about this?"

I shrug. "They seem to have had a falling out."

"What's his name?"

"Tom."

"Yeah?" He jots it down. "Tom what?"

"I don't know."

"You're a friend of hers you said, right?" In Officer Vinson's mental Patrol Guide, women tell their friends everything. Most do.

"I didn't say I was a good friend. Actually it's Sachi who hasn't been the good friend, but now isn't the time to play 'blame the victim.' Actually this morning when she called to tell me about this, it was the first time she'd called in many months, and I would have blown her off but she was distraught and told me what had happened and asked me to come over. So I went over." *Which is more than Sachi ever did or would ever do for me.*

"I'll get the name from Mary Louise." Vinson clears his throat. "She didn't tell you nothing about who did this to her?"

"Just where it happened. Stairwell near the corner of Prince and Thompson Streets. Downstairs from a bakery."

"She looks okay, your friend. Don't get me wrong, I'm not passing judgment on her or saying she is okay, but it could've been a lot worse. Girl over on Jane Street, she wound up here last night covered with a sheet." He gets up. "Okay, I'm gonna talk to Mary Louise when she comes out of there while we wait for the evidence. You going in to be with her?"

"If they'll let me," I say, hoping the answer is no. I don't think I'm up to this. I've been thinking the wrong kind of things since I walked into Sachi's apartment. There must be somebody better trained to deal with this. *Someone who'd be more sympathetic.* "I want to make a phone call first."

Vinson waves me over to the bank of phones at the nurse's station. "Make it quick," he warns.

"Thanks," I say. "I will." No one but Quick will do. I press the numbers for his extension and this time he picks up.

"I'm at Beth Israel," I tell him, watching the two uniforms conferring in the corridor. "I'm okay. Someone I know was assaulted last night and wanted me to come in with her."

"I got your message and tried calling you there. Apparently you hadn't arrived yet. Guys from the Sixth show?"

"Two uniforms. They're right outside."

"Trish said it happened on Prince Street. Someone from the First squad is going to go over there, contact Special Victims, and then they'll be in touch with your friend. She give a good description?"

"I don't know what she told them so far," I see Mary Louise O'Hara, a.k.a. Scarlett, gesticulating wildly with her hands, like she's about to strangle somebody. *Sachi has that effect on people.* "She didn't tell me anything."

Long pause. "She wants to cooperate, right?" This isn't really a question, more like wishful thinking. I bite my lip so I won't come right out and say, *it would be a first.*

"She was just raped," I feel like I have to remind myself as much as him. "Maybe she'll say more later. When this part of it is over. I'll stay with her a while. Once the shock wears off, maybe she'll feel more like talking about it."

"See what you can do." It's not the first time Quick has asked me to bait a friend for information.

"You think it could be the same who...ABC..."

"I won't know what to think until there's some information to go on," he says. "Listen, it's busy in the house, I've got to go."

"I'll talk to you later," I promise the dial tone. Officer Vinson looks up as I come back into the corridor. O'Hara pushes a stray strand of hair behind her ear and signals me to go back in the examining room with her. "Is this what you were wearing at the time you were attacked?" O'Hara indicates the slip dress neatly folded and placed on a paper-covered counter.

"No, I put that on after."

Assured that she's not tampering with evidence, O'Hara can't resist lightly skimming her fingers over the dress, as if satisfying her suspicion that it's pure silk. "Where are the clothes you were wearing when it happened?"

"I threw them in the hamper."

"Sachiko, is there anything...you can tell me about him?" I have a feeling this wasn't the question O'Hara originally intended to ask.

"I told you, it was dark. He grabbed me from behind, pulled me down, raped me from behind, raped me in the behind..." Sachi wipes a tear from her cheek with a corner of the hospital-issue examining gown. I reach out and squeeze her hand.

"Did he wear a condom?"

"No," Sachi sputters. "No condom."

O'Hara writes things down intermittently. A white-jacketed Asian woman struts into the examining room. "I'd like to be alone with the survivor now," she says testily. Sachi looks relieved at the sight of her. I pause on my way out, expecting to be called back in the room, but it doesn't happen. Never mind what comes next, she won't have to endure any more of this. At least for now.

"I wonder what other evidence she destroyed," O'Hara grumbles once we're in the hall, out of Sachi's hearing range.

"Hey, Mary Louise, want some coffee?" Vinson points in the direction of the room behind the nurses' station. O'Hara nods.

"She said she wanted me to be *in* there with her," I protest, not so much because I want to be in there with her—I don't—but I suddenly can't understand why she bothered with any of this, period.

"I have to wait here for the evidence bag, but let me tell you, she made sure to destroy as much as possible,"

O'Hara exclaims, taking the cup of coffee from Vinson. "Goes and showers, douches with vinegar and water, throws her clothes in the laundry. Wonder if she put them in the washer yet."

"There are no machines in her building. I think she goes to a laundromat on Thompson Street. At least she used to. I can't see her going over there this morning though...she'd just showered when I came over."

"Maybe we'll luck out there. She said the guy didn't wear a condom. If we get the soiled clothes, we should find semen, hair samples, maybe fibers from the perp's clothing if he unzipped but didn't strip. We're not going to find nothing much on her. Maybe the anal swabs will show something if she didn't go all out and give herself an enema too."

"It's the First's case now anyway," Vinson reminds her. "Once the Vitullo kit goes to the lab, it's not your headache."

"Thank God." O'Hara crumples the cup. "It's bad enough when we've got a cooperative victim. Last night we got one who couldn't cooperate even if she'd wanted to."

"I told her about that," Vinson says.

"I already knew about that," I tell both of them. "I'm going to be with her for a while." I point toward the closed door of the examining room. "I'll try to get her to be more forthcoming. Maybe once this part of it is behind her. I'll try to get her through the interview with the detectives."

"It's not your headache, Mary Louise," Vinson reiterates. I wish someone would tell me this wasn't my headache. How much cooperation are the other investigators going to get out of Sachi, even with me present? Maybe if I keep reminding her that she survived the attack and another woman wasn't so lucky, I'll appeal to her sense of responsibility. I'm not sure how much of a sense of responsibility Sachi has. *She certainly dumped me in the past when I was in need.* This could happen to someone else if she doesn't tell the detectives everything she can. Or the rapist could come back to her for a repeat performance. I'll try whatever it takes to get her to talk.

I keep thinking about the way Sachi's apartment looked when I walked in. The only thing missing was yellow tape saying POLICE LINE DO NOT CROSS. And Tom. I have to ask her about that too. I don't know if I'm any more likely than the detectives to get answers out of her, but I've got to try.

4

"What are you trying to imply?" Sachi asks, hands on hips. "That I'm lying?"

"It looks like something happened here that you're not telling us about." Montalvo, the detective from the First squad, has obviously seen enough crime scenes and enough issues of his wife's magazines to recognize that Sachi's living room does not merit the Good Housekeeping seal of approval. "We didn't find anything outside to corroborate your story. Plenty in here though, so let's go back to the beginning." He points to an upended armchair. "This looks like a good place to start."

"I did that." Sachi says.

"You picked up all these chairs and tables and broke all these plates, huh? Little thing like you." He shakes his head. Sachi extends her foot and kicks a quarter of a dinner plate aside. "Don't go hurting yourself now," Montalvo warns her. "We got your clothes out of the hamper rolled up with the bed linens. That ought to tell us more." He coughs. "How about you telling us more?"

"I've already told you..."

A husky female voice croaks, "Basta, Monty." I turn around to see where it's coming from. A tall woman with skin the color of cappuccino swaggers past the doorway and into the apartment, peels off her nylon New York Liberty windbreaker. "Okay to put this down?"

"Yeah, be my guest."

She aims for the sofa, the only piece of furniture on that side of the room remaining upright, tosses it and misses. "I never was good with those foul shots. Come over here." She waves Sachi over to her and places her hands on her shoulders, like a conjure woman would, to heal wounds. "I'm Detective Gibson from Special Victims. First name's Kent. Like the cigarettes my momma used to smoke."

"Can't imagine what we'd be calling you, Gibson, if your momma smoked Camels."

"I actually prefer a nice Cohiba now and then," she retorts. "Now you tell me what happened to you, honey, then we see what we can do about it, all right? Would you rather talk in there?" She gestures toward the bedroom.

Sachi shakes her head vehemently. "Here's okay."

Something happened in there, that's for sure. Montalvo gestures for me to join him on the far side of the room. "She's lying," he grumbles so softly that only I can hear him, but both Kent and Sachi turn and scowl in his direction.

"Not lying," I say. *Just not telling the whole truth. Anything but.*

"Let's go in there," he indicates the bedroom again. I follow him. Once inside, he sniffs like a bloodhound and sneezes. "Cologne," he says. "Take a whiff. It's still here. The guy musta worn a ton of cologne. It was in the sheets, on her clothes. Smell her out there, *she* don't smell like that. *You* don't smell like that. I sure as hell don't smell like that." He flaps his arms like wings and I spot spheres of perspiration on his shirt. "You recognize that smell?"

Yeah, no sweat, but I know he's not talking about *his* smell. I shake my head.

"Something real fishy going on here and I'm *not* talking about the cologne. Someone did something to her she didn't want done—whether she wanted it in the beginning and changed her mind, she's not telling, but it wasn't how she said it was and if Gibson doesn't get her to open up about it, there's no case. What'd she tell you?"

"Nothing different than she told you in there. Guy took her on those outside stairs; she didn't see him..."

"And you don't believe her any more than *I* do."

"Sachi's never been much on rearranging furniture. Some of those chairs look like they weigh more than she does..."

"The boyfriend."

"Maybe."

"What's he built like? Someone who works for a moving company maybe?"

"I've never seen him."

"You're a friend of hers, you said, right?"

Here we go again. "We haven't been close lately. Since this...Tom came into her life actually. Some girls are like that. Blow off their girlfriends when a guy comes into their lives and then come whining when they break up. She was whining about more than just that, so I came. But I don't feel comfortable about this."

"No, huh? That makes two of us. If she's making up stuff, she can go down for filing a false complaint. Some irony, huh, the guy who did this to her walks around scot-free and she ends up in lock-up. Know how a pretty little thing like her would fare in detention? Geez, I hate to think..." He shakes his head. "But she can't be jerking everyone around like this unless there's been a crime committed, which we think there was, but we're not absolutely sure what crime has been committed because she's not on the level with anybody yet. Not even you and she got you into this."

"What happens next?"

"That's up to her. Maybe Gibson in there can coax the truth out of her with her big momma charm. She gets lots of practice. Girls of her own—three teenagers—talk about a nightmare! Probably screens all their wannabe boyfriends through BCI after hours to make sure nothing like this ever happens to them." He looks out the door. "Uh, Gibson got her hands on her hips in there, bad stance, don't look too promising. Tell Sachiko if she wants us to nab this guy to get in touch with us and come clean and pray he don't feel like coming back for seconds in the meantime. Maybe she should think about taking another route home and avoiding stairwells."

"Here's my card," I hear Gibson say, "in case you remember anything, Sachiko." She shakes her head at Montalvo. He pauses at the door, waiting for Gibson to scoop up her jacket. "Swear I've seen you before."

"You might have. I was in the First a couple of times late last year. Friend of a friend was murdered. Detective Quick handled it."

"Hat Trick. Yeah, he did a Callahan on us. On his way out when I came in, but there was overlap there." He takes a last disgusted look around the apartment and follows Gibson out. I close the door behind them. I turn to Sachi. "What are you going to do about this mess?" I pick up a metal chair and set it right side up.

"Later," Sachi pulls me away from the furniture. "Right now there's something else I want you to do for me."

"What?"

"Do a drawing of the guy who did it."

"You want me to what?"

"I heard you did a drawing of the guy who came after you last year. So I'm asking you to do one for me."

"That was different. I saw him. I didn't see this guy...I thought you said you didn't see him."

"As far as the police are concerned, I didn't."

"Why aren't you getting the police concerned?"

"Because they're not. Or wouldn't be if they knew."

"Knew what?"

"I knew who it was. He was wearing a ski mask, but I knew..."

"Who was it?"

She shakes her head. "Let's just say it's somebody I know, but I don't want to ID him. But if you do a drawing of him, the police might be able to spot him before he does this to somebody else."

"Was it Tom? If it was Tom, you can just give me a picture of him. Don't you have any of him? I mean, regular photographs?"

"He took them all when he moved out and no, it wasn't Tom," she says. "I don't think."

"You don't think?"

"I had a few drinks last night before it happened. I was kind of woozy. They hit me stronger than usual. I guess I hadn't eaten enough."

"Wouldn't you know?" I sputter. "Why did he move out?"

"I cheated on him," she says. "I haven't heard from him since."

"Whoa..." This is moving too fast for me. "Was it the guy you cheated on him with?"

"I don't think...I don't know."

"And now you want me to do a drawing of him even though all you saw was a guy with a ski mask on?" I shake my head. "Why didn't you tell the police who you think did it?"

She shakes her head. "No. That's not the way I want to go."

"You want to go with this picture you want me to draw...and do what with it, may I ask?"

"Make sure it gets circulated in certain circles so it won't happen to anyone else..."

"You don't know that. All I could promise is a picture that would be a likeness and I can't promise a very good one. I never had the pleasure of meeting him. Either one of them. There could be a case of mistaken identity and that could lead to big trouble for a lot of people including you. Think about it, Satch! Some guy who had nothing to do with you or anyone else could get beat up or worse for being a suspected rapist on the basis of a picture...I can't do what you're asking me to do, no way!"

Sachi's eyes narrow. "You can, you just won't."

"I won't unless I get some answers."

She juts her chin. "I'm doing the best I can. Do I have to talk about this? I really don't want to any more."

"You're asking me to do something I don't feel comfortable with. You'd better tell me more if you want..."

"Anal, okay? He'd wanted me to and I wouldn't so he came back wearing a ton of cheap cologne and got what he wanted and made sure it hurt like hell."

"Did he usually wear cologne?"

"Not that brand, not like that. He didn't want me to know it was him."

"So you're saying it was Tom?"

"I'm saying I don't know! I don't think so, but it could have been...I don't know...my head was spinning. Tom wanted back door and I didn't want to so I thought maybe he was so mad at me that he could have disguised himself and come back and got back at me—boy, I'll say—but I don't know."

"Did whoever it was have any distinguishing marks... scars, moles, that sort of thing?"

"It was dark."

"So even if he did, you couldn't see them."

"Delilah, I was so out of it I didn't know what came over me." She shakes her head. "The police aren't going to buy any of it, are they?"

"Guess again, Sachi, date rape isn't exactly unheard of. You didn't even give them a chance. You *lied* to them. Telling them it happened outside. It happened right here, didn't it? They *know* when they're being lied to; career criminals lie to them all the time. You have nothing on them, the stories they tell. The police took your bedclothes for analysis, you know, so it's only a matter of time before they ask you about whatever stains they find on them and match them up to whatever they found in you. He didn't wear a condom, you said so yourself."

"I douched. I think I told you all that too. Look, Delilah, you're the one who insisted on calling the police. Throwing business your boyfriend's way?"

"He doesn't need it. He's got enough business to handle." I feel blood rush to my face. I've never said anything to anybody about Quick being my boyfriend. I've just thought about it a lot. "Okay, let's say it was...someone you know. If he raped you, it's quite possible he'll do the same thing to someone else eventually, when he doesn't get his way. My drawing him, you circulating the drawing in some underhanded manner, isn't going to prevent that." I take a deep breath. "I'll do a drawing, but only on the condition that we turn it over to the police afterward."

"What do I tell them?"

"Everything you haven't told them up to now. They're going to know you lied anyway, Satch, the minute they find out there's semen on your clothes, in those sheets. Maybe you have some clothes around that you wore when you were with Tom...or the other guy...that you could give them for comparison."

"Oh, yeah, I should never have brought that blue dress I got at the Gap to be dry cleaned."

"Really, Satch..."

"Really, Delilah, it's not like I was wearing clothes when I was with him, you know? Or the other guy. It's not like I thought one day I'd be collecting evidence against him."

"I can't do the drawing until later, anyway. I've got an assignment to sub at a middle school in Brooklyn " I glance at my watch. "And as it is, I'll just make it." I back out of the apartment and shout, "I'll call you from there, all right?" before shutting the door.

5

There never seems to be a train lighting up the tunnel when you need one in a hurry, but today one *is* there and the doors close just as the red message at the turnstile commands me to swipe my MetroCard through again. And again. *Damn!* I drop my MetroCard and get shoved by someone behind me. I turn around to give whoever it is a dirty look and see a dark-haired young girl wearing a pleated white dress. Late for her confirmation or something like that, I'm thinking. How long is that dress going to stay pristine down here? She looks dazed. I pick up my MetroCard and get through the turnstile on the next swipe, then step out of her way. She swipes hers, too, her hand shaking.

I head for the public phone to my right to call the school I'm supposed to be at to say I'm running a little late. Nobody answers. I'll apologize profusely when I get there. When I turn back toward the platform, the girl is on her knees, her head bowed. She must really be late if it's come to this. I've never seen anyone kneeling on a subway platform before. She closes her eyes. Commuters make a part around her. A street person starts singing "The Greatest Love Of All" in front of the newsstand, palm extended, asking for handouts. Commuters make a part around him too. They're just obstacles, like the red, white and blue poles along the length of the platform. I turn back to look at the girl. Behind me I get a whiff of cheap cologne. The same cologne I smelled in Sachi's bedroom. I whirl around. Anyone here could be wearing that cologne. And a lot of it too. I'm at a disadvantage. I don't know who I'm looking for. Who here would be Sachi's type? Do I know Sachi's type?

I go over to the newsstand to get a bag of M & Ms, sniffling so much from the cologne that the news-vendor gestures to a pile of pocket tissues. "You got a cold? You want these too, miss?" I shake my head. My feet sense the vibration of the approaching train first and I start dropping change in my hurry to pay the vendor before I miss this train too. A scream punctuates the approach of the train. *Trains don't make noise like this.* I whirl around and see a man with his hands extended in front of him. I can't tell if he's been grabbing at something or pushing something. The girl in the white dress literally flies in front of the train as it hisses to a stop. I cover my eyes for a split second and then force myself to look around me. A crowd forms around where the girl was kneeling just moments ago. More people scream. A couple of people lean over the platform and gag. I turn away again. I don't want to believe what I think just happened actually happened.

"She jumped."

"She was trying to get away from that person who grabbed her elbow."

"It looked to me like he was trying to keep her from jumping."

"It looked to me like he pushed her toward it."

"Well, she's gone anyway."

"Call nine-one-one, someone, hurry!"

All of these accounts turn out to be soliloquies because nobody's here to question these people, not yet. I take several deep breaths. I've lost the urge to sneeze. Whoever was wearing that cologne is gone. I take a good look at the faces on the platform. Quite a few of them have a distinct greenish tinge, blending well with the mosaics of beavers on the subway wall. I imagine mine must look that way too. I hear the squawk of police radios on the stairway. Suddenly blue uniforms swarm the platform and start buzzing orders. "Okay, everybody, stay back, give the EMS guys a chance to get through."

"She's beyond EMS," one onlooker says.

"You a doctor, sir?"

"Uh, no..."

"Well then, stand back with everyone else and let someone qualified make that determination."

A few people back up toward the turnstiles. Another officer stops them. "No one's going nowhere just yet. We got a report this girl was pushed."

"She wasn't pushed. Looked to me like she was trying to get away from somebody and lost her footing."

"That ain't all she lost."

"People, I'm going to have to ask you to stay over there by the newsstand out of our way till somebody asks you some questions about what happened here."

A man standing next to me clears his throat. "I didn't see anything, can I go?"

"No one's going nowhere," the officer snaps.

"Candy, gum, magazines," the newsstand vendor chants in a heavily accented voice. "Get something to pass the time."

"We want to talk to you too," the officer says to the vendor.

I can't see beyond the wall of blue lined up along the platform. I realize I still have the bag of M & Ms clutched in my hand. I've lost my craving for them and it's so hot on the platform that I'm sure they'll have melted before I leave. I look around for a trash can to throw them in and see more scuffed shoes descending the stairs. Then I see someone that makes my hand squish the life out of that bag of M & Ms altogether.

"Delilah," Quick says as he starts toward me. "Did you see anything?" I have a distinct feeling just from the tone of his voice that he would rather I didn't see anything.

It may be more a question of what I smelled. I shake my head. "I'm not sure. I don't know if what I noticed would be very helpful."

"Try me," he says. Under other circumstances there is nothing I'd rather do. "Wait here. I'll want to talk to you at the station."

"I have to wait here?"

He nods. "Afraid so." He mumbles a few asides to a uniformed cop to his right and then turns back to me. "I can't say how long we'll be. We've got to talk to a lot of witnesses." He looks around. "As you can see. We want to talk to anyone who's handicapped and elderly first, so they can go. We don't want anyone having heat stroke down here."

Another detective saunters up to him. "Girl did an Anna Karenina, from what I understand."

Where did he come up with that? I wonder if an all points bulletin is going to be posted for someone named Vronsky. The uniforms start beckoning potential witnesses away from the platform, toward the benches against the wall and through the turnstiles. A detective sidles up to the newsstand behind me. A baby begins to wail loudly. "I got to nurse," his mother protests, pulling at one of the policeman's sleeve with her free hand.

He whirls around. "Hey, don't do that."

"I got to nurse. My baby hungry."

"Sit over there," he points to the row of benches behind me, next to the newsstand.

I look over at the pay phone, thinking I better call the school to say I'm not going to be able to make it, period, that they're going to need a substitute for this substitute, and probably call Heidi Obermeyer, too, to tell her to get another model, but the line is longer than the line to cash checks in banks the first of the month. I hate doing a no-show but expect everybody will understand. *At least I hope they will.* The girl on the tracks is never going to show up for anything again. I'm beginning to smell vomit. I don't know how long it takes for a dead body to start to smell and I don't want to find out. I look over at Quick who's deep in conversation with yet another witness. *How can he stand this, dealing with death all the time*? I start to walk farther down the platform, as far away from the mayhem as I can, until I can't go any further.

"Miss, where you going?" someone calls out. I ignore him.

Then, "Delilah!"

I reel around. Quick waves me back and points to the congregation of witnesses clustered around the news-stand. "I need air," I whisper to him, clutching my stomach. "I feel like I'm going to be sick."

"Okay, hold on, I'll get someone to escort you." I wish I could hold on to him, witnesses be damned. "I want to talk to you at the house, not here. I'll be there as soon as I'm finished up here." He keeps watch on me as he takes a uniformed officer aside and then says something to him I can't hear and gestures for me to go with him. I'd gladly follow someone into a cell as long as it meant getting away from this. But I'd rather it be Quick.

6

The house, as it's called, is a home away from home for the officers stationed there. There's no advertisement for Italian cheese on the roof of this precinct house, which is a good thing considering how my stomach feels right now. As I get out of the blue-and-white, I have to take a giant step over something green wrapped in cellophane that might have been cheese in a former life.

Then again, maybe not.

I notice an empty playground across the street. Apparently nobody in the neighborhood feels like playing or else they're engaged in indoor fun and games. Officer Jackson clears his throat and signals me to follow him past the ubiquitous green lanterns framing the doorway into the precinct. Everything inside—the faded paint on the walls, the blinking fluorescent lighting—makes me feel like I'm going to be sick. Jackson stops at a candy machine to his right. "Want anything?" he calls to me over his shoulder. "Juice, maybe?"

I clutch my stomach. "Uh...no, thanks."

"They may be a while."

"That's okay."

A candy bar rumbles down the chute after he deposits the change and he slips it in his pocket, but not before I notice it's a Snickers. "You gotta go upstairs and wait for them to come back." He signals me to follow him. He leads me to a door with a glass window that reminds me of the one in my building, only this glass is tinted dark, not unlike the windows of cars confiscated from drug dealers that cruise around the parks. "After you," he says and then slams the door behind him. The paint in the stairwell is two-tone blue. Either somebody couldn't make up his mind which color was better or simply ran out of paint and made do with what was provided out of the city coffer. *At least it's not green.* Officer Jackson catches my arm before I head up the next flight of stairs across the hall.

"Down here," he gestures to his left with a jerk of his head. "Squad room."

He gestures for me to go into a mostly empty room and leaves me there. An old air conditioner in front of one of the metal desks clanks and makes me think of a death rattle. The lone detective sitting at a desk at the far end of the room looks up as I come in the room. "Detective Quick's desk?"

He indicates the one in front of the air conditioner. "He's out in the field," he informs me.

"I...I know. I was a witness. I didn't want to stay in the field...I mean, station." I slump in a hard wooden chair and look at the accumulation of forms on Quick's desk. A partially filled-out pink form flutters to the floor. I pick it up and stare at it.

The detective behind me suddenly clears his throat. "You're not supposed to be reading that stuff."

"Sorry." I drop it on the desk just in time as footsteps resonate from the stairwell, an advancing army of detectives returning to the barracks with witnesses in tow. I look around, wondering how everybody's going to fit. Quick is the only one who's empty-handed. *Not quite. He's got me.* The other detectives confer, keeping their witnesses in tow all the while like pit bulls on a leash, breaking huddle every few minutes to make sure none of them are sniffing each other out. One by one, they give a "follow me" signal and leave the room. Quick stays.

"Tell me what you saw," he says, thumping a pen against the metal desk.

"It's more a question of what I smelled." I take a deep breath. Quick drops the pen.

"Cologne. The person standing near her when she fell was wearing a ton of cologne and it smelled just like the cologne I smelled in Sachi's apartment before I got there. I didn't see him from the front, just from the back when I heard her scream. His arms were out like this," I hold my hands out in front of me like I'm pushing a heavy load.

"Remember what he was wearing?"

"A sweatshirt, I think. Dark red. It was so hot down there—that's the only reason I remember, because I was wondering how he could stand to wear something like that. She was wearing a white dress..."

"We know what she was wearing. What else can you tell me about him?"

"It happened too fast. That's it. That...and the smell."

"The cologne."

The detective sitting behind him coughs. "Sounds like you'd better have her go through the scratch and sniff books."

Quick ignores him. "Anything else?" he asks softly, hopefully. I shake my head, looking away from him at the window. "Looks like it's going to rain. It's getting dark."

"It's getting late."

"Didn't anyone see anything?"

"It happened too fast," he replies. "Nobody else I talked to has mentioned the smell."

"Maybe I noticed it more because I smelled so much of it earlier in Sachi's apartment. But I can't imagine not noticing it." I notice that he's not wearing any cologne at all. The extreme heat would make all but the strongest scents evaporate. Usually he smells of something faintly minty. Maybe it's not cologne at all—just the tang of chewing gum on his breath.

The thought of it makes my mouth water.

"Would you recognize it if you smelled it again?"

I nod, half expecting he is going to whip out scratch and sniff books. I think about the perfume inserts stuck in fashion magazines that I tear out and toss in the garbage. Maybe I should try to help him out by flipping through *GQ* and *Esquire* at a newsstand on my way home and smelling some of those.

"That should narrow the field to a few hundred thousand," mumbles the detective sitting behind us as if he can read my mind. "We can call it the Aramis line-up."

"That puts you in the line-up in position four, Grumbacher," Quick snaps.

I whisper to Quick, "In that case, you can rule out Aramis." The mention of Grumbacher reminds me of charcoal pencils and the promise I made to Sachi to do a drawing of the person who raped her, who she may or may not know, only on the condition that I turn it over to the police afterwards, but I don't want to bring this up to Quick—not yet. "I'm sorry I can't be of more help," I say, my voice quavering.

"I'll check and see if anyone's mentioned anything to anyone else about the smell. It may be something," Quick sounds anything but convinced. A shriek echoes from down the hall, followed by the slam of a door. Quick stands up, a sure sign he's dismissing me. "I'll get you a ride home."

"I can walk. I'll be okay."

"I'll get you a ride home," he insists. "I'd take you myself, but I have more witnesses coming in." He glances at his watch, then back up at me. "Should be any time now. They said they had to get babysitters. I'll call you later," he mumbles sotto voce. "I don't know how much later it'll be."

"Whenever." I have a feeling it's going to be very late. I may get some drawing in yet. That is, if I don't get sick first.

7

The big red LED display on my alarm clock glows three-thirty when I get the call. I reach for the phone. "How about if I come over and fix that lock for you?"

"Now?"

"Do you want me to?" All at once he sounds hesitant and I want him to come over more than ever. This has everything to do with opening doors between us, not locking them. I pull on a pair of black cotton capris and pull my MOMA T-shirt back down over them and grab a can of WD 40 from under the sink, which I hold up to him at the front door when he knocks ten minutes later. "Defense mechanism," I whisper. "In case it wasn't you. I'm being careful."

"Someone could take that away from you in a second," he says and takes it out of my sweaty palm to prove his point. He follows me up the stairs and closes the door behind us, puts the can of WD 40 on the table. He looks so tightly wound I think that, like the Tin Man in *The Wizard Of Oz*, he's the one who needs the petroleum in his joints to loosen him up, except he's not lacking a heart as far as I can tell. This case has gotten to him. He looks worse than I've ever seen him. I want to ask him if he's found out more and I don't dare because I know he hasn't. I cheated. I listened to the news station before bed. I don't want to let on that I know that they don't know what happened yet. "Are you okay?" he asks.

"Better now than I was," I assure him. My knees have stopped wobbling; my stomach has stopped churning. When I got dropped off earlier, I spent the first half hour gagging in the bathroom thinking I was going to throw up, before I remembered there was nothing in my stomach to throw up. I called the school I've been hired to sub at but everyone in the office had left for the day. Then I left an apologetic message on Heidi Obermeyer's answering machine and collapsed in a heap on my bed clutching myself, hating the feeling of being alone after seeing that.

I'm not alone now and the person I most want to clutch is standing right in front of me. *If he could stand being alone after seeing that, he wouldn't be here.* "Are you okay?"

"There are some things you never get used to, Delilah. Seeing that. She was just fourteen. A month shy of her fifteenth birthday." He shakes his head. "I couldn't stop it. I couldn't do anything for her."

I don't know how he could expect to, since he wasn't there when it happened. "Nobody saw it coming," I say. His arm slips around my waist. I didn't see that coming either.

"Are you sure you're okay?"

"I think I'm starting to feel a lot better."

"I wish you didn't have to see that."

"I don't know how you stand it."

"There are times when I don't want to, but I have to. It's my job, you know?"

I know. There are some things about my modeling work that have made me uncomfortable, but undressing in a roomful of artists isn't the same as constantly dealing with dead bodies. His other arm pulls me closer to him in a hug and I feel the light pressure of his chin on the top of my head, then he leans down and kisses me on the lips. This is not the first time he's kissed me. A couple of times after we went out to dinner together, he gave me a parting kiss before he had to go off to check on his sister or got a call to go back to the precinct. Then he would shift into retreat mode, coming close, closer, and then pulling back, leaving me wanting more and wondering if he was purposefully jerking me around, if there was someone else in his life after all. I'd stopped in the drugstore once before one of our dinner dates a few weeks ago and bought a dozen condoms just in case.

Good thing I did too. The kiss becomes less tentative. I can taste the spearmint in his mouth and feel the smooth edge of his front teeth on my tongue. His hands slip deftly under my T-shirt and edge toward the clasp of my bra. I take a deep breath as he fumbles with the hook. "You want me to stop?"

"No."

I lose the sense of which way to back up to get into the bedroom. In the heat of the moment, I'm lost in my own apartment. He has to steer me, his lips not once letting go, his lithe fingers working up and down my spine, playing the discs like the keys on a Steinway. I topple backward onto my bed pulling him down on top of me. Just enough light trickles in from the kitchen area to see him as he stands up to unfasten his shoulder holster and slings it over the bedpost. As he unbuttons his shirt clumsily with one hand, he strokes me with the other. He peels off the shirt. I grope for the drawer under the table by my bed, but before I can even get it open, he fishes a foil package out of his pants pocket and places it on the table. Then his hands slide under my T-shirt again, pulling it up and over my head. This isn't the first time he's seen me without my clothes on, but I still feel as naked as I did that first time. Maybe even more. He's not drawing me this time. But this time I get to see him too. He gently eases the capris down to my ankles and tugs at them until they fall on the floor. I pull him back down on top of me, just wanting the closeness as a warm-up, building to a feverish bump and grind. His mouth easily finds nipples that stand out even in darkness like Braille. He makes me forget how self-conscious I am of them. I've fantasized about being with him for so long I don't know where to begin and don't want it to end. My hands play with his hair. He reaches up, intertwines my fingers with his, kisses them and then brings them down to his pants. I tug at the zipper. The noise of the metal splitting open seems loud enough to wake up Mrs. Davidoff next door. *She's probably already awake, listening.* I tune out my inner censor. The foil packet Quick tears open is almost as loud, an after-shock. I'm not sure whether I'm expected to help. When I reach down for his hands, I feel fidgeting and I wait for him to cue me. I don't have to wait very long. He rolls against me, teasing me with his hardness, his hands running up and down my body like he's frisking me and then inviting me to do the same to him. Our breathing seems as loud as a passing siren piercing the silence of the night.

"I want you to..." I gasp. I can't bring myself to finish the sentence. I rely on sign language, reaching down, coaxing him in. I haven't been intimate with anyone for many months. Every new lover comes replete with his own street map. Being in bed with Quick is like rediscovering avenues I've driven on for years and I don't want to take any short cuts. I'm content to simply squirm under him, wrap my legs around him to pull him in tighter, run my fingertips up the nape of his neck and through his hair and try to keep from pulling it. I start to moan his name and stop myself. I can't moan his name without confusing things. I don't want him to change anything he's doing. "Hat trick," I suddenly gasp as the room starts to spin. "Hat trick! Hat trick!"

8

"You're aptly named," I whisper to him after many hours of lying silently beside him. I'm not sure how many hours of sleep either of us got. I tossed and turned and when I'd look at him, I saw his eyelids flicker open several times. He frowns and I rush in to assure him that I don't mean to imply he rushed through things. "That was magic. A hat trick. Like pulling rabbits out of..."

He laughs. "That nickname has nothing to do with sorcery," he says. "It's a hockey term. When a hockey player scores three goals in a game, he's said to have completed a hat trick."

I roll on top of him. "I guess you can add one to the record books."

"I don't keep those kind of records." His hand cradles my butt and pulls me closer. "I got that nickname when I was on patrol. I cracked three cases in a short period of time. That's how I made detective." He nuzzles my neck with his lips. "Three times? Really?"

"At least," I assure him, wondering if his detective skills carry over into this department too—if these are grounds for interrogation. *When you're having fun, who's counting?* All I know is that I'm game for more and from the feel of things, so is he. And then his cell phone rings.

It's not just any ring but "Reveille," a wake up call if there ever was one. He stands at attention, phone to his ear, his brow furrowing. I roll out of bed and walk to the bathroom, giving him the privacy to finish his conversation. He follows me. "Missing person," he says. "East Sixth Street. Young female."

"ABC?"

"We don't know if it's connected with that or not. Her roommate reported her missing and she didn't show up for work." He finishes dressing as he talks, buttons his shirt and shoves his gun in his holster. "Business as usual."

"Never a dull moment," I sigh.

He shakes his head. "No, not here, that's for sure. "

I'm at a loss for words. Changing the subject would seem too flippant. Asking for reassurance would seem too needy. He steps forward and wraps one arm around me in a mini-hug. *Thank you, officer, that'll have to do for now, I guess.*

"Rough day," I whimper.

"You could say that," he says, his brows furrowing. "The girl in the subway station—Ripley—she was a student at GreenWood Middle School. Seventh grade. Isn't that the school you said you're subbing at?"

I gulp. "I didn't show up, so I may not be subbing there anymore."

"I think they'll forgive you, given the circumstances." He pauses at the door. "We still don't know if it was an accident or something more. I think it's safe to say there will be a police presence there."

"Will it be your presence?"

He leans in and kisses me. "Last night was fun. I'll call you."

The air rushes out of me when he walks out the door. If I were in a cartoon, a gigantic 'whoosh' would pop up in a caption bubble over my head. I turn on the shower and step in, wishing the water could wash away what I witnessed yesterday without the warm cozy feeling of the last couple of hours going down the drain. I know I'm going to have to get out of the apartment for a while to clear my head. My cupboards are just about bare so a shopping expedition seems in order. I dress hurriedly and grab my bag that says it's not a bag and lock the door behind me. When I turn around, I collide with Mrs. Davidoff, the neighbor from hell who probably refers to me as the neighbor from hell.

"Ex...excuse me," I stammer, wondering how much she overheard last night. Her silent glare tells me she heard quite a lot. "I'm going shopping down on Hester Street. Do you need anything?" I force a Cheshire Cat smile.

My offer seems to soften her features a little, but she shakes her head after a few minutes and goes back to glaring at me. I quicken my pace and walk away from her before she can say anything, down the stairs, feeling virtual daggers in my back. The door clatters as I shut it behind me. On my way to the subway station at West Fourth, my cell phone rings and I see Sachi's number three times in the queue of calls I've ignored since last night. I hesitate, scrolling up and down, then touch her number and wait for her to pick up. Only she doesn't. And I'm informed her voice mailbox is full. I wonder if she's okay. The more I think of what happened to Sachi, the more pissed at her I feel, but that doesn't mean I don't want her to be okay. I just don't think I can think of her as a friend any more. I don't think she has thought of me as a friend for a while now. Except when she's in trouble.

I scamper down the stairs to the subway platform and slide my MetroCard at the turnstile. It's hot down here; the unseasonable near ninety-degree temperature of the past few days has infiltrated the underground, belying the theory that heat rises. I'm feeling hot in other ways, too, still weak in the knees from last night. Last night was something else, last night was great, just like getting exactly what I wanted for Christmas as a kid, not socks. And the fact that Quick more than lived up to my fantasies creates a new bugaboo for me to dwell on: where do we go from here? Right now I'm going to Hester Street to pick up a few groceries and then to get some art supplies. The D train hisses to a stop at Grand Street and I climb up the stairs to street level where the stench is not so grand. I start heading down the block when someone taps me lightly on the shoulder. "Don't I know you from somewhere?"

I wheel around and see a thirtyish guy wearing a maroon Fordham T-shirt and a formidable smile. Oh shit, here it comes, he remembers me from an art class I modeled for.

"Didn't I see you at Court Street in Brooklyn?"

"You might have...I was there to straighten out some red tape regarding employment."

"I always remember a pretty face," he says, shifting his weight from one leg to the other. "But I don't remember having been introduced." He extends his hand. "I'm Keaton Jeffries."

"Well...uh....nice to meet you. I'm Delilah Price." I don't extend my hand.

"So where in the city do you teach?"

"I'm a sub," I tell him. "I just got an assignment to teach at GreenWood..."

"Middle School? Small big city. That's where I teach."

"Really? What a coincidence."

Like this whole encounter was a coincidence. A little too coincidental. After having been stalked last year, I'm cynical and suspicious. Keaton Jeffries looks cool and comfortable and definitely has the inside track on what it's like teaching at GreenWood Middle School, so it might not be a bad idea to pick his brain a little. Just a little.

"Where else have you subbed?"

"This is my first assignment," I confess with a nervous smile. "So please be kind."

"A virgin."

"Well, I guess you could say..." I clear my throat.

"You'll do fine. The girls can be a handful sometimes, but threaten to send them to detention and they settle right down." His smile sends an inexplicable shudder down my spine. "Most of them."

"And if they don't?" I'm thinking of fourteen-year-old Ripley Herrera. Was she a handful? I don't know whether he knows what happened to her or if he knew her or knew of her. Quick told me about her on the Q.T. for all I know, so I'd be on guard. But surely Keaton Jeffries must know if he's on the faculty there. Wouldn't he? In any case, he's not getting the info from me.

"That's what I want," he exclaims, pointing to a fruit stand manned by a Chinese man who looks like he weighs eighty pounds, if that. Lined up in front of him are what looks like pineapples gone Goth, spikey husked and drawing a lot of sudden attention. The vendor seems to recognize Keaton Jeffries and smiles as he comes closer. "Come look," he says.

"What is that?" My nostrils twitch at the sudden blast of a foul smell, like fresh vomit but worse.

"Durian. Nectar of the gods."

"People eat that?"

Keaton picks one up, sniffs it near the stem and holds it close to his ear and shakes it like a marimba. Satisfied, he proffers it to the vendor who plops it on a hanging scale. "Thirty dollar," the vendor says.

"Thirty dollars for one fruit?" I say.

"It's worth it," Keaton asserts. "If you're game, I'll have Nyugen here cut it open and put it in a container and you can have a taste."

"Um...no, thanks," I shake my head.

"How about going for a bite to eat—not necessarily durian—when we're done shopping here? " He flashes his broad smile again. "Informal orientation. I can tell you everything about teaching at GreenWood that you want to know."

"I can't," I say. "I have plans." Those plans include buying casting plaster and making ramen for two days worth of meals, but I don't feel compelled to let him know that.

His charming smile instantly disappears, like somebody reached behind him and turned off a switch. "Right. Well, see you Monday." He tucks the durian in its net bag under his arm like a football and backs away, turning into the growing crowd surrounding the stalls and heading north.

What was that all about? I shake my head and walk in the opposite direction, toward Canal Street, feeling like I'm walking away from an accident scene without reporting it. My internal alarm, almost always in caution mode, is thrust into high alert with lights flashing and sirens clanging.

9

I'm about to be schooled big time, I think, as the D train barrels out of the tunnel and hisses to a stop at the Twenty-Fifth Street Station. I angle myself to jump out the minute the doors slide open and hurry toward the exit, mentally checking off first-day-on-the-job things I have to do. Last night I didn't do any of those things because Quick came over again. I didn't expect him to, but he did and we got busy. I feel hung over but not from booze—hung over and weak-kneed and walking-into-things delirious. I wonder if anyone can tell what I've been up to just by looking at me. Especially that nun.

The school is a short distance away, just a couple of blocks along a tree-lined street with rows of white and beige and gray two-story houses behind wrought-iron fences. A caravan of yellow school buses with red lights flashing snake around the school, and parked a half block away is a white truck with a placard that says CHECK YOUR PHONES $1. The first of the girls disembark from the first bus, then the driveway becomes a sea of girls of all shapes and sizes, all with dark green uniforms, almost all with backpacks or book bags slung over their shoulders, chewing gum, texting. A couple of them stand on the other side of the driveway smoking cigarettes, watching me warily.

I walk by them and open the door and immediately confront a metal detector. I understand why it's there; I just wish it didn't have to be there. I pause, running a mental

53

checklist of what items I have on me that could trigger the machine and plop my keys on the desk to my left. A couple of uniformed girls shove past me and the female security guard who has been standing like a statue grabs one of the girls by the collar. "Julissa, you didn't check your phone at the truck. Hand it over."

"I don't have my phone today."

"I saw you texting out there. Don't lie to me, girl."

"I didn't have the dollar. I won't use it."

"Here. Now."

Julissa slams her Droid on the table and starts to stomp off but the guard reels her back by her backpack strap. "Slide the bag through the metal detector."

"There's nothing in there!"

"Fine," the guard says. "Prove it."

Julissa puffs out her cheeks and suddenly bolts, runs down the hall where another guard catches her and steers her back to the doorway. "That wasn't very smart, Julissa. Open the bag. Now." The guard folds her arms. Julissa unzips her bag with shaking fingers and the guard passes the bag through the metal detector, immediately setting off beeps. She reaches in and retrieves a Swiss Army knife with the blade extended.

"It's to cut my apple at lunch," Julissa protests. "The cafeteria knives don't cut it."

"To the office, Julissa. Now!"

I'm next in line and the guard gives my messenger bag a perfunctory glance as I pass through the metal detector without a whimper and gather my keys. "These girls..." she mutters, shaking her head.

"I was going to ask where the office is," I say, "but I guess I just have to follow Julissa."

"If you follow Julissa, there's no telling where you'll end up," says the guard. She signals to the girl behind me.

"All right, Mona, come through the detector with your bag now and it better not beep!"

I exhale once I get to the office and show my ID and claim the lesson plans left by the teacher I'm subbing for who turns out to have been another substitute. "She was supposed to be here again last Thursday and didn't show up," the receptionist says, "and that's when you were called and of course you didn't show up..."

"I was in the subway station when a girl fell on the tracks..."

The receptionist visibly pales in spite of her layers of foundation. "She was a student here," she whispers, but I don't imagine it's a secret any more. "A grief counselor is supposed to be here today and tomorrow to talk with the girls, those who need her." The receptionist looks over my shoulder and I turn around and see Julissa watching us, her lips pursed, a smudge of wetness in the corners of her eyes. "The substitute just never showed up and we couldn't reach her." She shakes her head.

I can't help but wonder if she had a class filled with Julissas.

"Maybe she realized teaching wasn't for her?" I offer feebly.

"She taught here before," the receptionist says. "Many times. This is highly unusual."

A young woman with caramel skin and honey hair, wearing a loose snakeskin-pattern T-shirt dress slithers by and nods to Julissa. "You behaving yourself?" she asks with a concerned smile.

"Do I ever?" Julissa replies.

"Good point!" She turns around and smiles at me. "Hi, I'm Frederica Shaw. I teach math."

"I'm Delilah Price and I'm the art sub," I say as I offer my hand.

"Oh...another sub." Frederica seems momentarily taken aback. "Has anyone heard from Deidre?"

"Not a word," the receptionist shakes her head.

"Let me show you to your room. It's not too far from mine, in case you need anything." Frederica pauses at the door. "I'm sorry about Ripley, Julissa."

"Th...thanks."

"She was a good friend of hers," Frederica murmurs after we walk out of earshot. "I suspected she'd act out after this. Not that she hasn't before. Hopefully she'll talk to the grief counselor when she shows up, if she doesn't get suspended first."

"She had a Swiss Army knife in her backpack."

Frederica furrows her brow. "At least it wasn't a gun. We've had those too." She leads me down the hall and around the corner, past a row of lockers. "In there," she gestures. "It's not a lion's den; you'll be fine."

Student art covers the back wall, a collection of Warholian self-portraits and still lifes and landscapes. Some of the girls are doodling in the margins of their composition books when I walk in the room, while others are just slouching in their seats, moving their legs around, looking bored. "Hi, I'm Miss Price and I'm your substitute teacher for today," I say, my eyes flitting from one face to the next. I'm not sure if my smile disguises the tension I'm feeling in my gut. I'd rather be in my studio sculpting but I had so many teachers in my past who made no secret of the fact that they'd rather be anywhere but in the classroom that I feel I owe it to these students to at least be here for them, mentally as well as physically. Before I've even looked at the attendance sheet, another girl ambles in, snapping gum feverishly, sweeping her hair out of her eyes like she's swatting flies. A huge swath of her otherwise black hair is dyed Day-Glo purple. When I start calling out names,

I'm not surprised when she raises her arm when I call out "Violet Velez."

"Ultraviolet," a voice from the back of the room snickers.

"Fuck off!" she retorts without turning around.

I clear my throat and pick up the eraser behind me to clear off the blackboard. "I want us to loosen up. What I want us to do is..."

A knock on the door disrupts my train of thought. Just as I dismiss it as corridor noise, I hear rapping again, louder this time, and the door opens and Keaton Jeffries walks in. "How are things going in here?"

"Fine. They're going fine. Aren't they, girls?" I turn to them. Several are looking out the window or down at the floor.

"I have to go to the bathroom!" Violet Velez announces without asking permission to leave; she just ups and hurries to the door and slams it behind her.

"We're just starting to get to know each other. It might be better to ask me that at the end of the day. Or the end of the week." Or never, I think.

"Well, all right, but let me know if you need any help here," he says, "seeing as how this is your first time." He nods with a shit-eating grin that I have the urge to wipe off his face with the eraser I'm clenching in my hand.

"I certainly...won't," I say as the door closes behind him. The girls' expressions soften somewhat, maybe pitying me for what they know they are going to subject me to. Violet comes back in the room, looking both ways. "Are you okay, Violet?"

She nods. The other girls seem to exhale in unison, a chorus of unspoken relief. I wonder what Keaton Jeffries has done to "help" in the past that makes young girls shudder in their seats and need to run down the hall to pee.

10

"So how has your morning gone so far?" Frederica Shaw asks me as she slides her lunch tray down the table in the teachers' break room.

"Meh!" I throw up my arms in mock surrender, but it's pretty close to how I feel.

She giggles. "They'll get better when they get to know you."

"When they get to know me...Frederica, am I going to be here that long?"

"Freddie," she says. "Call me Freddie. Deidre, the last sub, is a missing person. No one's seen or heard from her since last Wednesday. It's not like her. She's subbed here before. She got along with everyone and everyone got along with her."

"Everyone?" I'm thinking of Keaton Jeffries.

"Well, as far as I know. Deidre is really chill."

"Who was she subbing for? Will she be back?"

"She's on maternity leave, so not for a while." Freddie picks at her salad with a plastic fork. "Don't worry, you'll do fine. These are some pretty tough girls. They haven't had it easy."

"Who has?"

"No one here, that's for sure."

"Did Julissa get suspended?"

"No, reprimanded. Due to the circumstances. She met with the grief counselor all morning, that's why she wasn't in your class. Ripley was a good friend of hers, like I said." Freddie takes a sip of juice. "And this was a terrible shock to us all."

"I was there in the subway station when it happened," I say.

"Oh, my God!" Juice sloshes over the rim of Freddie's glass as she lowers it. "What I heard is that either she fell or she jumped, but I don't think anyone here really knows. What did you see?" She puts up her hand. "I'm not sure if I want to know."

"I didn't see much. One minute she was there, the next minute she wasn't and people were screaming. Is there any reason why she'd jump?"

Freddie shakes her head. "She probably had less reason to jump than some of these other girls. She had decent grades, she had a supportive family, she was well liked, and she wasn't constantly getting into trouble like some of the others. She was a good influence, I'd say."

"Is there any reason somebody would want to push her?" I ask.

Freddie finches, like I just punched her. "Is that what happened?"

"I don't know. It's just a theory I heard discussed. The police haven't been here yet?" I'm not sure if I should be saying any of this. I'm not sure I should be telling her anything or even conjecturing. Freddie's friendliness has made me let down my guard, which isn't necessarily a bad thing unless I'm compromising the police investigation.

"I haven't seen any police here," Freddie says. "I'm not sure how the kids will react to that."

"If any of them know of anything that could have pushed Ripley to the edge..." I wince at my choice of words. "Something that could have been behind this, I'm sure they'd want to help?"

Freddie nods. "Some might. But some also see the police as the enemy. Some have seen family members arrested, have been harassed themselves. Whether they did something to deserve it or not, they're not likely to be too cooperative. I hope they won't pressure them..."

"I'm sure they won't," I say, though I'm not sure at all. It's something I want to ask Quick. There are a few other things I want to ask him, too, mainly concerning Keaton Jeffries, who struts in the room, banging the door behind him, giving a perfunctory nod at Freddie and plopping on the patched Naugahyde couch that looks like it was part of a restaurant booth in a past life. A thirtyish woman in silver-framed glasses comes in the room carrying a tray that she sets down at the far end of the table.

"Done handing out Kleenex for the day, Maya?" Keaton asks her.

"Don't be giving the grief counselor any grief, Keaton," Freddie snaps. "Excuse me, I have to go do some paperwork."

"I have to go too..." I say without excusing myself. I catch up with Freddie in the vestibule leading to the main corridor outside the cafeteria. Freddie's stiletto heels click on the floor like staccato exclamation points.

"He pisses me off so much!" Freddie mutters.

"He came in my room and offered to 'help,'" I tell her. She looks up at the ceiling, summoning divine guidance. "Do the girls have a problem with him?"

"You noticed."

"It's hard not to. What is it about him? Even when I met him Saturday, he rubbed me the wrong way, like..."

"You met him Saturday?" Freddie frowns.

"In Chinatown. I was shopping and he was shopping and he said he remembered me from somewhere. Corny. He said Court Street, but I was only there for a few minutes and I don't remember seeing him there." I shrug. "But I don't think he's as memorable as he thinks he is."

Freddie looks both ways and licks her lips. "I think we should get together after work one night this week to talk, away from here. There are a few things bothering me, but I don't want to say anything here...." The teachers' lounge door opens a crack. "I look forward to seeing what you've got the girls doing in there. Have a good rest of the day."

11

When I come out of school a little before three, I notice a dark Crown Victoria parked at an angle in front of the driveway and I realize I probably missed Quick and his partner by just a couple of minutes. They're in the office, I'm guessing, talking with the principal, the grief counselor, and whoever else they think might be able to tell them what would drive a fourteen-year-old girl to jump in front of a 6 train. She was definitely, as I overheard one detective say Friday, deep-sixed.

Unless she was pushed.

To think this is only the beginning of the week. I nod to one of the girls I recognize from class and she nods back and heads down the street, peeling off the uniform jacket and rolling up her sleeves. I spot some kind of tattoo. Out of nowhere Julissa runs up to her, whispers something in her ear, and they make a mad dash down the street and around the corner. When I turn back to the school, I see Keaton Jeffries standing by a side door smoking a cigarette, in clear violation of the sign that states NO SMOKING WITHIN 100 FEET OF ENTRY.

He doesn't see me and I want to keep it that way. I head in the opposite direction, even though it means walking extra blocks to get to the subway station. I see a girl walking halfway up the block and spot the fluorescent purple in her hair as she sweeps it back, even from this distance. Despite the heat, she hasn't peeled off her jacket. Looking at her makes me feel hotter. "Violet!" I call out. She tenses and wheels around, as if expecting some kind of assault. I extend my hand like I'm trying to calm a skittish puppy. "Are you okay?

"Why wouldn't I be?" She pales and then signals that she wants to keep walking. I keep pace with her, glad I'm wearing flats.

"Don't you want to take off your jacket? Aren't you hot?"

"I don't want to get it dirty," she says.

"I'll probably be teaching your class for the week at least, maybe longer," I say. "I'll be here if you need me, if you want to talk, just so you know." I hesitate. "Did you know Ripley?"

Violet glares at me. "I hated her," she says. Certainly a different picture from the one Freddie painted of the girl who was loved by all. Maybe not all.

"Why?"

"I have to go home now," Violet turns away from me and hastens down the block, swinging her backpack by the top handle. At the corner, she turns around and then continues walking south.

Fine, I want to go home now, too, I think. But I'm meeting my friend Morgan for a bite to eat at Madison Square Park first and then modeling for Heidi Obermeyer's class. As usual I'm running late and I'm going to be even later because of my elaborate detour. I haven't had much of a chance to see Morgan lately and I miss the days when we would get together like this for a burger or maybe meet at a dive bar and share shop talk and talk about guys. We're not talking about guys these days; Morgan's not crazy about the idea of me being involved with a cop and I'm worried about his loosey-goosey love life since his live-in partner was murdered last fall. When I see him waiting for me, I feel an indescribable sense of relief and also the need to vent.

Morgan orders a mushroom burger and I order a plain burger with lettuce, tomato and pickle. We both order an ale. "So what's the latest on Tokyo Rose?" he asks.

I roll my eyes. "I haven't talked to her since Friday. It may suck to say this, but I don't think she was raped at all. I think she was drunk and took this... whoever he was with the strong cologne...home with her and regretted it in the wee hours which is when she called me and the police for good measure, just for show."

The buzzer placed on the table between us suddenly flashes and vibrates. Morgan jumps up to get our order. "Your fine cuisine, ma'am." He slides my tray in front of me.

"If I did that, I'd spill it. Which is why I'm teaching and not waitressing, though I've been second-guessing that career move all day."

"Fun day at work?"

"I can't begin to tell you." I take a bite of my burger and a gulp of my ale.

"It's only temporary."

"Most assuredly."

"You're molding young minds."

"Actually a few of those minds need mold removal. Might have to call the HAZMAT unit. The detective squad is already parked there."

"Really? How handy for you."

I let that one pass. I dunk a French fry into a pyramid of ketchup. "One day at it and I feel like an abject failure."

"You're never an abject failure at anything, darling."

"Oh, you're so sweet!" I jump up and kiss him, then freeze. "Oh, shit, would you believe I'm still afraid to show affection publicly after last year?" I look to my left and right. Lots of people are here; they're only interested in what's on their trays. I hope.

Morgan waves it off. "Don't even think about that any more."

"I can't help but remember. Vittorio was killed because of that."

"I'm just glad you weren't killed too."

I blow a kiss discreetly. "Are you going to finish those fries?"

"With a little help. Where are you heading after here?"

"Have a class to pose for, then home. I'm so beat. I hope I'll be reclining." I stuff a fry in my mouth. "I have to contact a gallery that may be closing before I even get any of my work in there. Whatever work I have to show."

"You'll get it done."

"Even if it's in my sleep, yeah, I'll get it done."

"You gotta do what you gotta do."

"Hey, I did meet a couple of nice people there today." I say brightly. And a real turd. I shudder at the thought of Keaton Jeffries. Freddie Shaw suggested that we get together sometime this week after work and I'm going to take her up on that sooner rather than later.

12

I show up early for my evening stint in Heidi Obermey-er's class, only a couple of blocks south. The new window shades are lowered, much to my relief; no police cadets across the street are going to get an eyeful of this class. Heidi struts in, as punk as ever, and gives me a big hug. Her hair is still dyed purple. What is it with purple hair? She looks like she could be Violet Velez's older sister.

I haven't modeled nearly as much as I used to and I hope I won't disappoint. For a while I didn't model at all. Then I needed money too much to stay 'retired,' though the money I'm making doing this isn't nearly enough to get by, which is why I wound up applying to be a substitute teacher. If I waitressed, maybe I'd make more with tips. Back to that waitressing thing. I have to remind myself that when I waitressed in college, I lasted less than a week.

I still feel comfortable in my own skin once I've dis-robed and start to pose. I watch the students study me as they make quick pencil strokes, erase, smudge. Nobody seems to be sizing me up as anything other than a three-dimensional prop, which is the way it's supposed to be. But I wonder what the faculty of GreenWood Middle School would make of this picture, not to mention the students, not to mention their parents. It's none of their business, of course; I'm not modeling for them. But I think they'd think more in terms of a Penthouse pin-up than a Picasso muse, a common misconception of the non-art-oriented. Nobody in this class has any middle-school-aged kids, I think; I'm safe. But they could have nieces or cousins or sisters.

I haven't even told Quick I've started modeling for art classes again, though he never said anything about it and I never volunteered any information about it other than "just the facts." It's nothing he has any say in anyway. It's not like I know everything about his life. All I know is what he chooses to tell me. Modeling for this class feels liberating, a chance to shed my inhibitions as well as my clothes and late spring is the very best time to be doing this, comfort wise. No need for space heaters.

"How are ya doing?" Heidi asks me during break. "Ah'm sorry you couldn't make it here last Friday, but ah perfectly understand. How do ya get mixed up in all these predicaments anyway?"

"Just lucky, I guess?" I shrug.

"You're doin' a fine job. Haven't missed a beat."

My cell phone doesn't miss a beat either; I hear it in my messenger bag from halfway across the studio. "Excuse me," I say to Heidi as I walk over to retrieve it. Quick's cell phone number lights up. "Hi," I lower my voice.

"I won't be able to come over tonight," he says. I didn't expect him to come over every night, but I feel like a pin stuck me and I'm deflating a little. He didn't have to call to tell me that, I remind myself. I wonder what he did call to tell me. I hear outdoor noises in the background, the insistent blips of a siren in the distance. "I'll call you tomorrow," he says and I barely have time to say "Bye."

Shit, that was quick.

Heidi glances at her watch. "If you need a couple of extra minutes break, that's okay," she reassures me.

"Thanks," I take a deep breath.

"You seem distracted," she says.

"I guess you could say that. I'm working as a substitute art teacher at a charter school in Brooklyn and I'm thinking of some ideas to engage my students." So they won't kill each other.

"Have them do selfies," Heidi suggests. "And make storyboards about themselves."

The idea is so mind numbingly brilliant that I'm shamed by my inability to think of anything half as clever. Someone like Heidi should be teaching at GreenWood, not me. I guess I should have looked for a waitressing job. What's spilled soup compared to feeling inept in front of a classroom of unruly pubescent girls knowing somebody else would do a more bang-up job than me?

"I love it! There's only one problem," I say. "They're not allowed phones or cameras in the school. They have to check them at a truck parked outside."

"Bummer. Can't you tell those farts it's for a class project?"

"I'll see what I can do," I say. "Or maybe I'll just take pictures of them myself…if they let me in with a camera."

13

It turns out that the school computers are going to take the girls' selfies. "It's the best we can do, Miss Price," the principal tells me, instructing me to take the girls to the computer lab for their PhotoBooth portraits at the start of class, then print out the results and bring them back to our classroom. I'm actually looking forward to seeing the girls take a stab at this, hopefully not literally.

Julissa walks in the room first. She seems subdued, not at all like she was yesterday, maybe because of her session with the grief counselor or maybe because she has something else up her rolled sleeve. The other girls strut in, slinging backpacks off their shoulders, eyeing me warily. Violet is the last girl to stumble in and ease into her chair.

"What I want you guys to do- yes, I know you're not 'guys'- is to come with me to the computer lab for a few minutes. We're going to take selfies and then use the pictures to make a two-part storyboard, one side showing how you see yourself and the other side showing how you think others see you. You can work on this for as long as you want to."

Julissa raises her hand. "Why can't we use our phones to take our selfies?"

"This will be as much fun," I say, knowing I can't very well say 'I asked, but they wouldn't let us.' After a hurried roll call, I ask the girls to follow me en masse to the computer lab down the hall. A bank of computers lined up against the walls flickers to life as the girls drum on the keys and enter their passwords. I direct them to the PhotoBooth feature but some have already accessed it and start playing with special features. "Take a few photos that you like and then we'll print them out and bring them back to class so you can work with them there." I watch as the printers start to hum and spit out image after image. I'm not sure what to expect, especially when I hear some of the girls burst into giggles. I hope they're not doing anything that'll get me fired on my second day. Or maybe I do.

I feel fraught with tension during the trek back to our classroom, expecting another nasty encounter with Keaton Jeffries, but the only people in the corridors are custodians and police. They're not in uniforms, but I can recognize police in plain clothes- or perhaps even lack of clothes- in my sleep. And then I see Quick heading in the front office. I herd the girls back into our classroom and close the door behind us with a none-too-subtle slam. The girls seem oblivious to everything but their selfies, clutched in their hands. "In back of the room are poster boards. Take one and put your picture in the center. On one side, put images that reflect how you see yourself and on the other side, images of how you think others see you. You can draw or use collage. I brought in some magazines for you to get pictures from to get started, but since you'll be working on this for a while, you can bring things in from home too."

"No Cosmo?" Julissa scowls as she flips through the pile.

"Afraid not," I say.

She pulls out a copy of *People* and heads back to her desk. The other girls yank at the magazines, knocking several on the floor. Violet stands back, waiting for the leftovers. There are none. "I have something here," I volunteer, holding up a copy of *Seventeen* that I saw in a desk drawer when I opened it to stash a hastily wrapped sandwich, an issue still bearing a faded address label. "Violet, would you like this?"

She extends her hand tentatively. "Thanks."

I vow to myself not to butt in on the girls while they're assembling and cutting out pages they want to use for their boards. They're in it for the long haul. My thoughts drift back down the corridor. What's Quick doing here?

I hear the staccato clicks of heels outside the door and more doors slam. And then I hear a loud cry. "Oh, noooo!"

The girls look up quizzically. "What's going on out there?"

I debate the decision to leave the girls unattended for more than two seconds and just open the door a crack. I hear subdued crying. I know I don't want the girls to hear this. "I'll be right back," I promise, slipping out and closing the door behind me. I walk toward the office, trying to be quiet and not let on that I'm too far away. When I get to the office, I see Freddie sitting in a chair, head hanging down. Quick looks up at me. "What happened?"

"They found Deidre," Freddie says, not looking up.

"Was that...?" I'm about to say, 'Is that what you called me about last night and decided not to tell me?' But that would be TMI. Nobody here needs to know my private business, not even Freddie, at least not yet. "Was that the missing substitute teacher?" I stammer, knowing damn well that it was. I put my hand lightly on Freddie's shoulder. "Are you okay?" She nods slowly and then shakes her head. I look up at Quick. "What happened?"

"We found her last night in Inwood Hill Park. Body was positively identified earlier this morning."

"How..." Freddie murmurs. Quick doesn't answer.

"I'll meet you in the break room for lunch, okay?" I squeeze her shoulder. "I've got to get back to the kids." I look back at Quick, but my questions are going to have to wait.

14

"She was strangled and stuffed in a garbage bag," Freddie murmurs shaking her head, her plastic-wrapped sandwich untouched in front of her. Nobody else is in the break room, just us, but Quick and another detective are still in the school, questioning others who knew Deidre and even some who didn't. I don't know what to say. I reach out and squeeze her hand.

"What did the police say?"

"Oh, not much. They seemed more interested in what I had to say. Which wasn't much either. Not enough to be of much help, I don't think."

"You never know what could help," I say, mimicking what Quick has told me more than once.

"I guess," Freddie stares down her sandwich.

Approaching footsteps make us both tense. Quick comes in the break room and stands near the door. Am I imagining it or did Freddie just flinch? "Have either of you seen Keaton Jeffries?"

"No, I haven't. I think he must have taken a personal day," Freddie says. "If he were here, we'd have seen him, no question. Did you ask in the office?"

"Nobody seems to have heard from him or knows where he is."

"A blessing," sighs Freddie, slowly unwrapping her sandwich.

"I'm inclined to agree," I add. Freddie nods.

"Mr. Popularity," Quick says. "If either of you do see him, let us know." He holds my gaze a few extra seconds and turns on his heels and closes the door behind him.

"Us? I only saw one of him," Freddie says. "And not a bad one at that," she adds softly. I feel my face flush.

"All for one and one for all. They think like a team." A hockey team if it were up to him. I feel like the air has been sucked out of me. "How well did Keaton know Deidre? They did know each other, didn't they? Because, I mean, they both taught here."

"I think they went out a couple of times. Casually. I already told that detective that. Probably why he wants to talk with him. "

"How did he act with her?" I prod. "When they were here?"

"All right. Keaton was always his usual asshole self and Deidre teased him and I think that charmed him, turned him on to her. He liked to see how much she could put up with. Turned out, she had her limit. She started to date someone else. And so did he."

"Who?"

I expect Freddie to say 'I don't know.' She drops her sandwich mid-bite. "Me."

"You..."

"A couple of months ago. And only once. I broke up with him too. He's an insufferable prick, really. Me! Me! Me! He's probably moved on to three girls by now. He's probably with one of them right now. Personal day indeed."

"Where do you think he'd go?"

"To the ocean or to the park. Or to a movie or bowling alley or the moon—who knows." Freddie shrugs. "I didn't mislead the police, if that's what you're thinking—he could be anywhere. I wonder if..."

"What?"

Freddie shakes her head. "I was going to say, I wonder if Keaton had something to do with what happened to Deidre. He's an asshole, but I don't know if he's a murderous asshole."

"You never know what some people are capable of," I say woodenly. I know that all too well. "The police are on it, Freddie. They'll talk to him—once they find him, that is—and maybe he has an alibi." Or maybe not. "You said Deidre was dating someone else. Do you know who?"

Freddie frowns. "Not by name. I didn't get the feeling she was head over heels, but I didn't really see her much here, she was subbing at another school for a while. And then, when she was supposed to be here last week...she wasn't."

"Can you find out who he was? As for Keaton, just let them know if you see him or hear from him. Or let me know." I hurriedly write down my digits on a piece of scrap paper someone conveniently left behind. The bell marking the end of another class jars me. "That's supposed to be a seven," I point to the last number that shot upward when the bell made my hand jerk. "Call me if you need anything, okay?"

15

What I need is a hug, but I'm not getting anything from Quick tonight but his voice mail message. I click on 'end' and can't help but wonder if it is the end. Logic tells me that his ongoing investigation takes precedence; after all, I'll still be here when he catches the ABC guy—if he catches the ABC guy. Or will I? How does he know I will? Does he care if I will?

Sex fucks up everything. So does lack of sleep. I can't think clearly. I make sure the door and fire escape window are locked and turn the rinky-dink air conditioner on high and stand in front of it to aerate myself before climbing into bed. The relief lasts about five minutes. My cell phone rings and my heart races when I see the number. "I'm out-side your door. I knocked. Are you in there?"

I bolt out of bed and throw on an oversized T-shirt and dash to the door, then hesitate and take a deep breath. Cool down. I slide the chain lock, turn the deadbolt, and open the door a crack. "Hi," I say, trying to approximate a sexy hoarseness. Quick is having none of it right now. He looks like he just saw a corpse. And perhaps he has. I step back, tripping over my own two feet, giving him room to enter. "So what's new?" I try to read his face, as usual an inscrutable mask when he's in cop mode.

"We spoke with Keaton Jeffries. He claims to have an alibi for his whereabouts at the time Deidre Marx disap-peared," Quick says. "Thing is, we hadn't even asked him if he had one yet."

"So did it check out?"

"We're working on it."

"He gives me the creeps," I say.

"How so?"

"The way he acts with everybody in the school. The way the girls act when they see him. The way he just so conveniently bumped into me on Delancey Street over the weekend before I even started working there."

"You didn't say anything about this before."

"I didn't think it was important before," I say. "And it's not like you can file a complaint or a police report for somebody just showing up or being a smart ass. Can you?" I did enough of that in the recent past already.

"Keep a record of it. And any other things that you notice. Two people from the same school dying violently in a matter of days seems more than coincidental. And so does him 'bumping' into you. Keep a record of anything and everything you think we should know about—and even things you're not sure about." He leans in closer. "But don't put yourself out there."

"I'd rather be putting myself out here," I say.

His mouth sucks the breath out of me. When I come up for air, he takes a step backward, not the move I was expecting. "I can't stay. I'd love to, but I can't. We're working ABC around the clock. I'll call you." He turns to open the door. "And you call us if you've got something."

Oh, I've got something bad, I think, as I hear his footsteps retreat down the hall and fade out down the stairway. I still feel breathless. I realize I didn't tell him about Freddie having dated Keaton briefly, about Deidre having started to date a mystery man. I'll add it to the 'class notes.' I was thinking pleasure before business. It doesn't work that way with Quick. Probably not even if I'd answered the door naked. He's seen it all before.

16

I'm late to school and out of breath as I flick the lights on in the classroom just minutes before the girls start to show up. Julissa is first. She drops her backpack with a thud and fumbles with the toggles, eyeing the other girls as they arrive in staggered fashion and then seems to beam as she retrieves her poster board. I'm not sure if that's a good thing or not. Violet, as always, is last to come in.

"How are we doing with our boards?" I ask, knowing it's way too premature to expect to be seeing much. My rank inexperience is as conspicuous as the sweat stains under my arms. It's only 8 a.m. It's going to be a long day.

Julissa gets to work right away, juggling colored pencils and clipped images from magazines. The others bow their heads over their boards and draw with number-two pencils and erase. Violet stares at her blank board. When she moves her arm over her board to cover up its blankness, her sleeve moves and uncovers slight red marks and Band-Aids on her wrist. I'm reluctant to butt in any more than I already did the other day when I intercepted her on her way home, but this is going in the daily record, not necessarily as something I'm going to share with Quick. More like the school psychologist, if there is a school psychologist.

"I'd work better if I could listen to some Drake," Julissa scowls, eyeing me uneasily, holding up her iPod Shuffle.

I shake my head. "Sorry. You can do that when you're working on it at home. And how'd you get that past the security desk?"

"Guard was distracted. You're not going to take it away?" Her eyes narrow.

"No," I say. "No, I'm not. But you're not going to play it."

"I'd work better if I had something to eat. I didn't have breakfast," says another student who I hesitatingly recognize from yesterday's seating plan as Aubrey, though she's sitting in a different seat. She holds up an energy bar. "I have Type-1 diabetes. I could die if I don't eat this."

I have no way of knowing if she's telling the truth but why would she lie about something like that? I nod. "Okay, Aubrey, under the circumstances, but neatly please." The look she gives Julissa makes me think she foiled me but it's not like I can make her submit to a glucose test.

I wonder what would make Violet work better.

Freddie isn't in the break room when I go in there after my next two morning classes which were a lot less fraught with tension and drama than the 'problem girls' class. Freddie isn't there but I haven't even had time to put cream in my coffee when Keaton Jeffries struts in.

"Alone at last, what a nice surprise."

I ignore him.

"I hope my not being here yesterday didn't cause too much trouble," he says. "A matter of a personal nature came up."

I'm not asking. I wish I could tell him his absence was barely noticed but that was far from the truth. Freddie comes in the room and pauses for a moment, like she's deciding whether to stay or leave, then sits at the far end of the table. Keaton takes a sip of coffee, staring at us over the brim of his Styrofoam cup. "Sorry to hear about Deidre, Freddie." he says.

"I'll bet you are."

"What do you want me to say?" Keaton slams his cup down, sloshing coffee on the table. "And since when were you such good friends with her? I seem to remember a few things that maybe you neglected to tell the police in your haste to cast suspicion on me."

"Ahem," I say. "Freddie didn't say anything to the police about you. I was there when she was talking to them." *Well, part of the time.* "They were talking to all the staff members, not just Freddie."

Keaton glares at me as if to say, Who asked you? Freddie smirks.

"What she said. They were talking to everybody here and wanted to talk with people who weren't here."

"Standard procedure," I add.

"And you know this because you're banging a cop?"

All the air whooshes out of me. He doesn't know, he can't know, but his conjecture hit bulls-eye. I labor not to react, not to give him any reason to think he's actually on to something.

"That's incredibly low, even coming from you" Freddie snarls, drawing his attention away from me. I gesture at the corridor with my head and she nods. "I need some fresh air. It's gotten stuffy in here."

"It's stuffier out there," he says. I open the door and lead the way down the hall toward the exit doors. Freddie's heels clicking on the floor provide angry punctuation.

"What a dickhead," she says.

I nod in acknowledgement. "Do you want to go out and meet me for a drink later? Or a bite to eat? Where we can talk in peace?"

"I could probably use all three," Freddie says. "Sounds good."

17

I'm sipping a light ale, milking it as long as I can, while I'm waiting for Freddie who is already more than a half hour late. Finally I see a pair of gravity defying stilettos descend the stairs leading down to one of my favorite watering holes. How does she walk so gracefully in those things? How does she walk in them at all? She squeezes through a gathering of guys who turn and watch her sway past. "I'm so sorry!" she exclaims, throwing up her arms. "I had to take a bit of a detour. I would have called but my phone was dead." Freddie takes a deep breath. "I need a drink."

"I need a refill," I say, signaling the bartender. "Let's grab a table. So we can talk."

"So much to talk about," Freddie gnaws on her lip.

"Is everything okay?"

"Wait until we sit down." She gestures to a wooden table across from the bar. A few men at the bar turn around to check her out and nod in appreciation. I hear one mutter "Nice piece of ass" in the tone of someone who knows he'll never grab that piece. I crook my finger and point to a table farther away from their line of vision. In my loose floral cotton overall, my shape is all but obscured by poppies and that suits me just fine. I plop the beer in front of Freddie and then realize I didn't even ask her if that's what she wanted. "Did you want something else? I'm sorry, I wasn't thinking...."

"Beer's fine. Place is fine. Rustic. Hey, they have popcorn!"

"I'll get us some." I eye the men at the bar warily as I hand over a five-dollar bill and gesture at the popcorn machine. The bartender plops a bowl of popcorn in front of me and hands me four singles. I rush back to Freddie and give her first dibs. She looks hungry.

"So, is teaching everything you expected it to be?" Freddie asks.

"I don't know what I expected," I confess. "I'm not a born teacher. I think I found that out on day one. But I'm fulfilling what was asked of me until the end of the school year. If I don't get fired first."

"They won't fire you. They need substitutes bad."

"Even bad substitutes?"

"I think you're selling yourself short." Freddie takes a sip of her beer. "At least you care about the girls and that's all they need. Give them something constructive to do and make them feel cared about."

"Do you know Violet is a cutter?" I whisper, as though we're still in school and someone might recognize names. "I saw the marks on her wrists and her arms. She hides them. I thought it was strange, her wearing her uniform jacket even after leaving school. Have you seen them? Has anyone else said anything about it?"

"She's not the only one," Freddie says. "There are some who are bulimic too. And other things. Lots of troubled kiddies at GreenWood. The real bad ones go to see Dr. Zimmerman. He's an adolescent psychiatrist in Bed-Stuy. The kids go to see him in his office, the ones who need to, but of course then sometimes they're no shows."

"They don't like him?"

"They don't like confronting their demons, as you can tell."

"Speaking of demons..." I gesture at the small crowd at the door in front of the bar. Standing slightly apart from the group of what looks to be college guys is Keaton Jeffries, wearing a baseball cap with a big red B on it, smirking seemingly to himself, drinking a dark beer. "What the fuck is he doing here?"

"Trolling. I don't believe it." Freddie slides down in her chair. "He hasn't seen us, has he?"

"Not...yet." I sink down in my chair too. "If I weren't already so paranoid, I'd swear he's stalking us. And being paranoid, I absolutely swear he's stalking us."

Freddie finishes off her beer. "Why are you paranoid?"

"I was stalked. Last fall. Not that very long ago. Not long enough ago. Is he still here? I wish he'd leave, I need another beer now."

"I'll get you one."

"I'll get you one," Keaton offers, thereby answering my question. "It'll be my pleasure. You too, Frederica?"

Freddie pushes her glass toward him rather than make hand contact. When he turns away to walk to the bar, she turns to me. "We could still leave and go somewhere else. Stiff him for the drinks."

"He'd see us."

"The reason I was late was that I saw him. I didn't think he saw me and I thought I lost him. Guess not."

"Freddie, is there more you're not telling me? About him, about him and you?"

"Later," she says, warning me with her tone that he's approaching fast. Keaton places the glasses down on the table and sits down next to me. "I think I owe you ladies an apology for how I've been acting lately. I've been distracted. My mother's been sick. That's why I took a personal day yesterday; she was admitted to Mass General again and I drove up to Boston to see her."

"How is she?"

"Stable."

"What's wrong with her?"

Keaton's reaction tells me I've crossed the line. "They don't know yet. They're still running tests." His mouth twitches.

"Well, I'm sorry, Keaton," Freddie says. Her face looks earnest. I probably look anything but. I don't know what Freddie would think of me if I act like I think Keaton is full of shit, which is exactly what I think he is. Maybe she does, too, but if so, she's putting on a better act than I am. "I lost my mama a couple of years ago so I know what you're going through. I hope yours will be okay."

"Thank you, Frederica," he says, shooting me with a 38-caliber stare for not responding in kind. I just take a long sip of beer. How long is he going to grace us with his presence anyway? "How about a nice game of darts?" He gestures to the dartboards on the wall in back of the bar. "A chance to unwind and release some of our hostilities." He winks at me. He's calling me hostile?

"You're on," Freddie slides off the bench and struts in front of Keaton who stops to collect the darts from the bartender. A group watching the baseball game on a television near the bar eye Keaton warily. He squints at the score and smiles. "Five to zip Sawks, all right!"

"I think there's going to be a barroom brawl tonight," I mutter to Freddie, gesturing at Keaton's ass with a carefully aimed dart while his back is turned.

"Hold that pose and wait until he turns around," Freddie whispers.

"You're bad," I say approvingly, but her reference to pose takes me aback. Freddie doesn't know about my posing for art classes, at least not yet, not that I know of, not from me anyhow, but I do believe I'll tell her now that I know her well enough to know she'll 'get' it.

"You know how to play?"

I force a smile. "I'm a fast learner."

"I'll bet you are."

I take aim and fling my darts in quick succession, landing them on 1, 2, and 12, missing 3 by the breadth of a fingernail. I mutter "Shit!" as Keaton hits his marks effortlessly. Freddie goes next. Keaton gestures toward my glass. "Do you want another drink, Delilah?"

"Trying to get me drunk?"

"It's an enticing idea, but then if I did you might kill me with those things."

"She might anyway," Freddie says. "Figuratively, of course."

I fire away at 3, 4 and 5, hitting 3, 4 and 12. "Two out of three ain't bad," Keaton smirks. "You sure you didn't already have too much?"

"All right, get me another."

"You sure about that?"

"Yes. Get me another." I wait until Keaton turns his back and heads to the bar and then I reach for his empty beer glass and wrap it with a paper napkin, before slipping it in my messenger bag. I see Freddie looking at me quizzically. "Did anyone else see?" I whisper.

Freddie shakes her head. "I don't think so. What are you going to do with that?"

"DNA," I whisper as Keaton heads back in our direction with a full pitcher. A leggy redhead intercepts him. Thank God.

"He's going to want to know where his glass went." Freddie slides her glass in front of me. "Mine, but he doesn't have to know that. I don't want any more. Are you sure you do?"

"No, I'm not—I don't," I admit, feeling queasy from the beer I've already drunk and the tension of being way too close to a person I loathe. "I think we'd better get out of here. How the hell are we going to get out of here?"

"Pretend you're feeling sick."

"I don't have to pretend very hard," I say.

"Hey, look, Keaton, I have to get her outside for some fresh air; she's not feeling so good," Freddie says, gesturing to me. I groan on cue.

"The air's probably fresher in here than out there. There's something like eighty percent humidity out there."

"Put your arm around my neck, Delilah. I'll help you." Freddie urges me, balancing my weight admiringly while maneuvering backward in her Jimmy Choos. "Excuse us, please,"

"But I just got a fresh pitcher!"

Freddie flashes him a devilish smile. "Bottoms up!"

We retreat to the door. I throw in a couple of extra moans and stagger for effect. Just before Freddie shuts the door behind us, Keaton bellows, "You owe me."

18

"You make a good wingman," I tell Freddie when we finally stop at the front steps of my apartment building. I keep looking behind us but now I'm sure that Keaton hasn't followed us. "But how do you fly in those things?"

Freddie laughs. "The same way you fly in *those* things." She gestures at my Vans. "I do get down and dirty sometimes. Like when I'm helping Habitat do a house. Can't do that in these. But anything else?" She smiles. "Plus they make marvelous weapons if some creep corners you." She kicks up a heel. "You think?"

"Absolutely." I nod. "But we don't know any creeps, do we?" I jerk my head in the direction of the bar we left.

"I'd better be getting home. It's a school night."

"Are you going to be okay?" I look down the street again. "It's you he was following, Freddie. Does he know where you...oh, right, he does know where you live, doesn't he? You said you went out with him."

"I'll be fine, Delilah. Honest. Hopping right on the D train at West Fourth and I'll be home in a half hour or so. See you tomorrow morning." She smiles. "Don't worry."

"Well, call me when you get home safe," I implore her. "Please?"

"All right, mama," Freddie laughs. "I'll call."

Before Freddie walks ten steps away, a dark sedan turns the corner and pulls up to the curb. She stops in her tracks when Quick leans out the window. "I was here earlier," he says. "Your neighbor said you were out."

I don't have to ask which neighbor he's referring to. He nods to Freddie and she flashes me a quizzical look. She looks nervous, too, and I want to tell her she has nothing to be nervous about but I can't because I don't know that. "Did you get a call from your friend Sachiko earlier?" Quick asks me. I almost ask, *who*?

"Sachi? No...no, I haven't heard from her since last week when she was...you know."

"She's in the hospital. Took pills."

I'm more concerned for Freddie, still standing a few feet away, not sure what her role is in any of this. "Are you sure you'll be okay?" I ask her.

"I'll be fine," she says, though less assuredly than before. "Will you?"

"Yes," I say. "I'll see you at work in the morning. Call my cell when you get home." I call to her retreating figure. I walk around the front of the car and get in without being asked and turn to Quick. "How bad is she? Sachi? Is she..."

"Resting uncomfortably. She'll be fine. We had a few follow-up questions for her. She'll be more uncomfortable when we go back to finish asking, if she doesn't give us the answers we want."

I nod. *Serves her right.* "Freddie seemed uncomfortable just now. Was she questioned too?"

"Not by me, not since I came to the school the other day, though I can't promise we won't want to talk with her again or anyone else at the school who we already talked to."

"I like her. A girl needs a BFF." I swear I can still hear her heels clicking from a block away. Most of my friends have been guys. Aside from Sachi, who proved not to be much of a friend at all; she's a poster child for why I've always trusted my male besties more. I felt different tonight though. While we were taking Keaton on in the bar, I felt like Freddie and I could be the 2000s version of Thelma and Louise. And now I'm looking at Quick warily, like he might scare her off with his intense policing, just as he drove a wedge between Morgan and me for a time. He and I still don't talk about that. It's a healed wound, but there's still a scar. It's hard to know what he's thinking. As usual. "One other thing," I say, reaching in my bag and retrieving Keaton's beer glass, the napkin still wrapped around it. "DNA sample of one Keaton Jeffries."

"What?"

"When he wasn't looking. When he went to get a pitcher." I hold it out to him. He doesn't take it.

"Even if this matched anything we found at a crime scene, it wouldn't be admissible. And there's nothing linking him to any of the crimes we're investigating yet."

"The operational word is yet."

Quick drums on the steering wheel with his fingers. "What makes you think he has anything to do with any of this?"

"What makes you think he doesn't?"

"I didn't say he doesn't. But why don't you leave it to us? If he saw you and things got ugly, he could wind up getting jammed up for something, you know that. Not to mention that you stole the glass."

"And the napkin. Are you going to take it or aren't you? I don't want it. I don't want to drink out of his scuzzy glass."

"How much did you drink tonight anyhow?"

"A few too many," I admit.

He takes the glass from me, napkin and all, and carefully places it in the glove compartment. "It's a school night."

"I know all too well," I nod.

"Why don't you go upstairs and call it a night. You can talk with Sachiko tomorrow afternoon." It may sound like a suggestion, but I recognize it as an order. I'm not looking forward to talking with Sachi tomorrow or any other time, drunk or sober.

I get out of the car and hesitate. "Do you want to come up?"

"I can't," he says with a sigh. "I have to go back to the house." It's not home he's talking about and I know it. "We'll see you tomorrow. Go on up. I'll wait until you're inside."

How long I'll have to wait until I see him again is anyone's guess.

I whip out my phone and check for messages as I go up the stairs to my building, looking both ways again before I let myself in, even though Quick is parked right at the curb. Force of habit. I tiptoe up the stairs so I won't disturb Mrs. Davidoff, who is apparently peering through her peephole. I hear rustling behind her door. "Good night, Mrs. Davidoff," I call out to the rustling and it stops. After I've closed my door, I check my phone again. How long does it take Freddie to get home? Then I remember Freddie said her phone was dead. I guess I'm not so drunk after all. We still need to talk, away from the girls, away from school, away from Keaton Jeffries. There's something she's not telling me, like Sachi, only she's nothing at all like Sachi, which is a blessing. I just hope she made it home okay. As I told Quick, I need a BFF.

19

Whether the school needs substitutes bad or not, I feel shamed when I walk past the office to my classroom late. Somebody had to take attendance for me. Somebody had to turn the data in to the office. I am so screwed. Or maybe not. My relief is so absolute when I see Freddie walk out of my room that I literally feel my stress whoosh out of me with my breath. But Freddie doesn't look happy. I wonder if she's pissed off at me.

"Violet's missing," she says before I can apologize. I feel like I've been punched in the gut.

"Missing as in absent?"

"She never came home yesterday," Freddie says. "Her grandmother called the school to ask if she was here this morning, but she's not."

"And she didn't call anyone else to report this?"

"She apparently said she thought she might be staying with a friend."

"She doesn't have friends," I say. "As far as I've been able to tell."

"Well, Abuelita Teresa apparently doesn't know that. So she's been missing since yesterday afternoon as far as anyone knows." Freddie shrugs helplessly. "I wanted to give you a heads-up."

"What do the other girls know?"

"Nothing yet, I don't think. Or if they do, they're not letting on. I'll catch you during lunch, I've got to get back to my class."

"I'm really sorry I was late."

"Oh, stop," Freddie says, patting my arm. "You're here. No problem. I'm glad I could cover." She doesn't look too glad, though, and I'm not sure if it's because of Violet being missing or me being so late that she had to cover. But she's clearly giving me a bye.

I love you, I mouth to her retreating figure. Drinking too much beer last night is a piss poor excuse for my having been late; she drank at least as much beer as me and she got here on time. *But she lives in Brooklyn.* My hand grips the doorknob to my classroom and I take a deep breath. *What am I in for?* I exhale and stride in, trying to maintain an assertive air. I feel like I should burst into a refrain of "I Have Confidence." Every day I seem to be doing worse. I should be sculpting. I should be a barista.

Julissa wheels around when I walk in the room, her hand gripping an eraser. The other girls cover their mouths with their hands, muffling guffaws. I get a glimpse of a crude drawing of a girl before Julissa hurriedly erases it and claps the chalk off her hands.

"Self portrait, Julissa?" I ask edgily, turning the table on her. I know Julissa was depicting Violet and she isn't present to defend herself. I'm hoping she's present somewhere, period. I don't think Julissa or the others would be crass enough to ridicule Violet if they knew she was missing. Or would they? "Please be seated and start working on your boards. Everybody."

"I left mine home," Aubrey says.

"Fine. Fine, Aubrey. Just take another piece of poster board and plan ahead; think what you're going to add to it when you get home and next time you bring it. I hope you are working on these at home too?"

"Like we don't have enough homework already," I hear somebody mutter.

"Home is work, Miss P," Julissa chimes in. "It's more relaxing being here. Just sayin.'"

That's a frightening thought. I look out the window and see a blue-and-white parked outside, near the phone truck. I hurriedly turn my attention back to the classroom, not wanting the girls to catch on unless they need to. I take a deep breath. The door rattles and opens. I expect to see a uniform but it's Violet who struts in, avoiding eye contact. She ambles to her desk and drops her backpack at her feet. The other girls look up. I hear a cough, a chortle, assorted whispers, then the rustling of heavy paper.

"Could we get busy?" I say and it's not a mere suggestion. I want to steer attention away from Violet, whose head is bent over her poster board, her hand making measured pencil strokes. Wherever she was for the last several hours, she had her poster board with her and was apparently working on it. Impressive. *Let that be a lesson, Aubrey.* I resist the urge to cop a peek or say anything to her, at least until class is over. My worst fear, that she cut herself maybe a little too deep, wasn't realized.

Where was she?

Julissa starts singing and jiggling her feet under her desk. I look to make sure she's not listening to her forbidden iTunes but her desktop is apparatus-free and there are no buds in her ears. I don't know if there's an edict against singing and even if there is, I'm not enforcing it. Violet crouches further over her storyboard, blocking the rest of the world out, something the other girls aren't doing.

"Hey, Lissa, could you change the tune?" Aubrey asks.

"Fuck off!'" Julissa snaps at her. "This is my inspirational music." She looks up at me and adds, "Since I can't listen to it silently on my iPod."

"Could you watch your language, at least?"

"Anyone here not hear the word 'fuck' before? Guess not." Julissa shrugs. "I'm sorry if I offended anybody."

The bell makes me jump like I've woken up from a bad dream. Julissa throws her pencils in a zipper compartment, stashes her storyboard in her backpack and swings it over her right shoulder, smacking Violet's elbow.

"Bitch, watch where you're going!" Violet cries out.

"I'm sorry," Julissa says, sounding anything but. Violet rubs an eraser over a smudge on her board with Lady Macbeth ferocity. I wait until the other girls have left and then I inch closer. I want to sneak a peek at her work, hoping to gain a clue to her disappearing and reappearing act. There are hands, huge hands, coming up at her from behind, hands hovering near her breasts, hands sneaking under her pleated skirt, nothing but hands. *Whose hands are they?* She quickly shields it from view as she stashes it in her backpack. "Violet, is everything okay?" Lame, I think, everything is anything but okay.

She looks up at me. "It will be." She gathers her things and scoots past me toward the door.

"You had everyone worried about you."

"Everyone? I'll bet."

"Wait, Violet. Please...wait."

She stops but doesn't turn around. I don't feel I can physically restrain her. I take a deep breath. "If you want to talk...tell me anything, I'll be here."

The door slams in my face.

20

"Whose hands?" Freddie looks aghast.

"Man hands. Big man hands. No face. At least not yet." I shake my head. "And now I don't know if she'll finish it. Because she saw me look."

"Did she say where she was since yesterday?"

"No, she didn't say much of anything and I didn't ask. I feel like I'm walking barefoot on broken glass. If I make the wrong move, say the wrong thing..." I shake my head. "Has her family been notified that she's okay? Though okay is relative..."

"I hope so. I hope somebody called her grandmother at least. She at least cared enough to call. And I'm glad she came back. I began to think...well, you can guess what I began to think." Freddie shakes her head. "There's just so much you can do. Just keep reasonable order and hope for the best. Want a cup of coffee? After last night, you probably need it."

"After last night, I can probably use a whole pot but... not now." I spot Keaton Jeffries approaching from down the hall and have the urge to hide. As he comes closer, my gaze drifts down to his hands.

"Ladies," he says, implying by his tone of voice that he'd rather be calling us something else. "It was lovely seeing you last night."

"The pleasure was all yours."

"Oh, that one hit bulls-eye," he smirks. "Why'd you two stiff me the pitcher of beer?"

"You mean you didn't find someone else to share it with you?" Freddie asks.

"I didn't say I didn't."

"Then we owe you nada." Freddie gestures for me to follow her down the hall. I turn around when we reach the water fountain; Keaton mercifully stays behind.

"Douche," Freddie whispers.

"Dickhead," I mutter. Freddie gives a thumbs-up.

"I feel like I should I talk to someone about Violet." I look both ways to make sure nobody can hear us. "Do you think that child psychiatrist, Dr. Zimmerman, would talk to me?"

"Not about anyone directly. Doctor-patient confidentiality. But maybe he can suggest how to proceed with an anonymous troubled student."

"Good point. I'll call," I tell her, wondering even now what I'll say. I'm not a relative. I'm not an administrator or even her regular teacher. But the front office's take on the situation was, "Well, she's here now." The school nurse complained that she barely has the authority to dole out Band-Aids and certainly can't get into the kids' psyches. What's the worst thing this Dr. Zimmerman can say?

"I'm sorry, but Dr. Zimmerman isn't in the office," the receptionist says when I finally reach the right Zimmerman. "He doesn't have any appointments today. Who am I talking to?"

"I'm calling about a missing child," I say.

"Are you sure you have the right number? What does this have to do with Dr. Zimmerman?"

"She's a patient of his."

"Are you a referring physician?"

"Well, no..." I stammer.

"Dr. Zimmerman isn't able to disclose information about patients."

"I'm afraid she could be a danger to herself..."

"Who are you?"

"I'm a teacher and the girl is my student."

"Except that she's missing?" the receptionist sounds like my 'Who's On First' routine might make her need a psychiatrist.

"I know she's a patient of his. I just wonder if he could say if she's a danger to herself." I lick my lips. "Or others." Sometimes you just have to push the envelope to get results.

"I'm going to put you on hold," the receptionist says acidly and promptly hangs up on me. When I call back I get a prerecorded message. I hesitate, wondering if I should leave a message, but decide I'll call back in the morning when Dr. Zimmerman will presumably have appointments. I plop my phone back in my messenger bag and look up to see Violet glaring at me. Did she hear anything? Maybe, maybe not, but she did see me with my phone.

"Violet, can we talk?"

She turns and dashes out the door.

"No, I guess not," I say softly to myself. "Wait...wait... Violet, you can't leave, school's not over for the day. Violet..." I run to the door and watch aghast as someone in a hoodie drapes his arm around Violet and corrals her, leading her to a waiting junker of a car, its passenger door yawning wide open. I run outside, not sure if I'll even be able to get back in and start toward Violet, but she scrambles into the car and the guy in the hoodie slams the door, glares at me, and runs around to the driver's side and jumps in. "Stop!" I yell at the retreating plume of smoke heaving from under the car, making it almost invisible as it careens south. "Oh, Violet..."

21

"She went willingly, didn't she?" Mrs. Wimbish, the principal isn't even posing it as a question in reply to my report that I called 911. "She was reported missing this morning, then she shows up, then she takes off before classes are over for the day and gets in some dude's car. It doesn't sound like an abduction to me. This is characteristic of Violet."

"Or it could be she's running away from a bad situation and maybe getting herself into a worse one," I suggest.

"Was he restraining her in any way?" the school guard pipes in.

"He put his arm around her," I say. "And then she got in the car. But that doesn't mean it wasn't under duress. She made these drawings...of hands coming at her."

"Whose hands?"

"No face, I'm afraid, just hands. Big man hands."

"Let's see these drawings."

"She has them with her...in her backpack. Unless she left it in her locker, but I don't think I've seen her without that backpack since I started teaching her. She was even working on it wherever she was before she came to school this morning. But I don't remember if she had it with her or not—I was focused on her."

"What was her assignment, exactly?"

"I told the girls to use mixed media or whatever they wanted to depict how they see themselves and how they

97

think others see them." I take a deep breath. "It seems to me Violet feels she's under attack. And she might be in danger. And I can't believe my calling nine-one-one about it is a problem."

"Having one student commit suicide and a teacher turn up murdered is a problem." Mrs. Wimbish replies acidly. "There's already a strong likelihood that GreenWood will be one of the schools forced to close in the near future and another scandal will almost certainly close our doors. And it would be a shame if it were over a false alarm."

"Yes, a damn shame!" I snap sarcastically, knowing I'm teetering on the brink of unemployment. "It'll be a bigger shame if no one does anything and Violet turns up dead. That'll really be a problem!"

The squawks of a police radio in the corridor stop any more of Mrs. Wimbish's squawking. I have to make an exit, so that I can go to the hospital and somehow cajole or badger Sachi into telling a closer version of the truth about what happened to her. I feel like one of the students, asking permission to leave detention.

A voice in the corridor says, "In here, officers." The two uniforms who stride in look like they'd rather be anywhere but here. "Okay, who's missing this time?"

"Seventh grader named Violet Velez," says Mrs. Wimbish. "Repeat truant. Late arrival and early dismissal today. Miss Price here says she saw her fleeing with a boy in a car."

Officer Salerno turns to me. "Was he using force?"

"He put his arm around her."

"Cozy. Did he push her in the car, did she try to resist?"

I shake my head. "He could have been verbally threatening her."

"What kind of car was it?"

"I didn't get a really good look at it," I confess. "It was dark. Dirty. Smelly. Loud."

"What direction did Shitty Shitty Bang Bang go?"

I pause. "South, I think."

Officer Salerno nods. "Wrong way on a one-way street on top of everything else. Has her family reported her missing? It could have been a family friend."

"It didn't look that friendly. And the family did file a missing person report," I protest. "Her grandmother called to report her missing and ask if she was here this morning before she got here."

"And I called her back and told her she was here," says Mrs. Wimbish, glaring at me.

"Did anything unusual happen in class today?"

"Aside from her being missing for eighteen hours before coming to class today, nothing more than usual, but I'm not her only teacher, so I don't know what happened in any other classes. Just mine. The other girls give her grief. She seems to dish back but..." I shake my head. "Violet's a cutter," I say. "She's in danger, if not from this...boy, then from herself. Why aren't you taking this more seriously?"

"We are taking it seriously. Maybe we would take it more seriously if Violet didn't have a history of this behavior, Miss Price. You're a substitute teacher," Mrs. Wimbish reminds me. "A substitute for a substitute. You're not their social worker."

"And the substitute I'm substituting for was murdered. And a student too."

"Ripley Herrera committed suicide," says Mrs. Wimbish dryly. "None of these incidents are connected."

Your opinion. I can't say anything. I just nod, biting my lip to keep from getting myself in even more trouble. Mrs. Wimbish hands Officer Salerno a school photo of Violet. "She's short, black hair...well, mostly black, she dyed some streaks violet," Mrs. Wimbish pauses for effect. "Brown eyes, a little chubby."

Officer Salerno pulls a mini notebook out of his pocket and jots some of the info down and shoves the notebook and photo back in his pocket. "Let us know if she turns up again." The staccato bell announcing the end of classes for the day makes him jump. "Long time since I've been in school," he chuckles.

"She's done this before," Mrs. Wimbish reiterates, looking squarely at me. "I wouldn't be surprised if she shows up in school tomorrow. For however long."

I back out of the principal's office, feeling again like a chastened freshman caught passing notes. I can't say I'd be terribly upset if I'm told not to come back. But I'd be disappointed to not see the girls' project to fruition and I'd miss hanging with Freddie. I'd be very upset if something happened to Violet. Too much is going on at this school to be coincidental. And I'm thinking that Mrs. Wimbish knows a lot more than she's letting on.

22

"You don't know that," Quick says when I fill him in when I arrive at the hospital to try to shame Sachi into telling some version of the truth. He was schmoozing with Detective Gibson from Special Victims when I stepped off the elevator. She nods at me and excuses herself to use her phone.

"She's more concerned about saving her ass than her student body," I point out. "And I think she could be covering up things. What school administrator shrugs off missing and dying students?"

"A school administrator who has a lot at stake. We've talked with Principal Wimbish."

"What did we find out?"

He flashes me an are-you-kidding look. "Let's see what you can find out," he says, nudging me toward the partially closed hospital room door. Sachi is propped up in bed waving her hands, not to welcome anyone but to try to speed dry a freshly applied coat of polish. She doesn't even smile. *What am I doing here?* I guess she knows why I'm here.

"How are you?" I start to sit on the side of the bed, then check myself and slide into a roughly upholstered chair across from her, as I would with somebody contagious. Quick has left us alone, at least, knowing I'd get nothing out of her if he or Detective Gibson stayed within earshot.

"Have you made up your mind what really happened to you last week?" I ask point-blank.

"That's a sucky thing to say."

"Lying about what happened is a sucky thing to do. Did you get raped or not? A few people have been raped. A couple...maybe more than a couple were murdered. You might be charged with obstructing justice if you lie." I remember Quick threatening me with that very thing in the past. "So what happened? That subterfuge about the guy wearing a mask, did it really happen that way?"

Whatever friendship was between us is dead now. Her eyes focus on the flickering images on the television in the corner.

"Suppose you tell me what he looks like so I can do a drawing?"

"I thought you didn't want to do that," Sachi snaps.

"It might be instrumental to finding out who did it," I suggest. "I'd like to know what he looks like myself. In case he's this ABC rapist they're looking for."

"I told you, I think I know who he was...but I don't remember his name. Or if he told me his name. I had a one-night stand with him. And then he turned up at the bar I went to that night and I think he must have followed me home. I was out of it. I think he may have put something in my drink, but I can't be sure."

I grip a number-four pencil in my left hand and begin to draw as Sachi recounts vague facial features. Narrow face, no, not *that* narrow. Squinty eyes. Nice nose. I frown. "He wasn't wearing a mask, was he, Sachi?" She clams up again and I hold up the rough drawing, just outline pencil strokes. "Color hair?"

"Light brown," she mutters.

"Eyes?"

"A little more farther apart. A little less squinty. Arched brows."

I'm beginning to feel slightly nauseous. "Mouth?"

"Full lips. More so on the bottom."

I'm biting my bottom lip now as I erase and redraw them. "What do you think?"

"Yes, that looks like him," Sachi acknowledges.

The drawing is almost the spitting image of Keaton Jeffries, so much so that I want to spit on him. I grab a glass of water sitting on the metal table next to the chair and take a gulp, not even thinking who might have sipped from it before. "Anything else you can remember?"

"No," she says, sliding down into the recesses of the bed. I'm relieved that I can hand this drawing over to Quick or Gibson and not have to look at it any more than I have to. I tuck it under my arm and open the door just wide enough to slide through. Quick and Gibson are at the far end of the nurse's station and look up as I approach them.

"What did you come up with?"

"This," I hold up my drawing. I still feel like I could throw up. "Remind you of anyone you know?"

Quick frowns. "This is what you came up with based on her description?"

"Are you insinuating that my personal suspicions influenced my drawing?"

"You said that. I'm not insinuating anything." He takes the drawing, stares at it, and then holds it out for Detective Gibson. She nods.

"Well?"

"We'll be having another talk with him, that's for sure," Gibson assures me. "But she's not pressing charges."

"He dated that other substitute, Deidre Marx."

"He had an alibi," Quick reminds me. "We'll be talking to him again. All right, Miss Prosecutor?" He seems almost amused by my fervor to hang Keaton Jeffries high; almost, but not quite.

"What about that beer glass?"

Quick's look stops me from saying more. "I told you that's inadmissible," he says, barely whispering. "And in any case, DNA would take time. Fingerprints, on the other hand..." He stands tall again, looking askance to verify Detective Gibson is out of earshot. "In any case, I wouldn't be alone with him."

"In any case, I wouldn't want to be," I say, adding sotto voce. "I want to be alone with you."

For a second there, Quick looks like he might lose it, might back me into a private room, or linen closet even, and take up where we left off last week, but that look suddenly turns dutiful when he sees the fast approaching Detective Gibson. "Ten-ten," she says. "A car reported stolen earlier just turned up in the Seven-Six, on Hoyt Street, empty, motor running, some kind of a hit list on the front seat. Students and staff at a school..."

"Let's go," Quick jerks his head toward the bank of elevators down the hall.

"What school," I ask.

"GreenWood Middle School," Gibson says.

Quick stops in his tracks and Gibson gestures for him to follow her. "There's a girl missing," I say. "She got in a car before classes were over and I'm afraid she could be in trouble." I'm picturing Violet. Was it that car? *Oh, Violet.*

"Are you going to be okay?" he asks me. Which was what I asked Violet this morning. Is everything okay? *It will be*, she replied. I just nod. "Yes, yes, I'm okay, just let me know if there's something I need to know."

Like if I'm on that hit list.

23

There's a definite increase in police presence near the school as I approach the CHECK YOUR PHONES truck, where a guard I haven't seen before is standing at attention. A junker of a car parked across the street with two shadowy occupants sitting in the front seat might as well have "Unmarked Police Car" flashing on its roof in neon lights. The girls huddle in small clusters sucking up their last few minutes with their precious devices before check-in time. I can overhear snippets of conversation, including "crazy bitch" and "I should've decked her" and I recognize Julissa's voice. I don't know how much they know about the school threat, aside from the fact that, "It's a fucking pain in the ass." Agreed, but I sure don't remember anyone talking like this when I was in seventh grade. *Did we*?

There's no sign of Violet or any indication that she's missing either. As far as I know, she's not being sought for anything more than accountability. Quick said he had nothing on her. I scoot by and hurry in the building, hoping I'll see Freddie before classes start for the day. I see her almost immediately, walking past the metal detector. "Any news?" I whisper to her when I catch up to her after passing through the scan myself, hoping that maybe the threat turned out to be nothing more than a hoax and the extra security is just a precaution.

"Nothing," Freddie says. "What do you know about it that you're not telling us?" Her tone isn't so friendly anymore, more like defensive and, not inexplicably, scared. I'm guessing she connected the dots leading from me to Quick. I almost lost Morgan's friendship because of my relationship with him. Is Freddie next? Before I can say anything, Freddie frowns. "Look, I've just got to ask—are you a cop?"

"Me? No!" I didn't expect her to think that. "Freddie, I'm, just...um... dating one." I wonder if that's a stretch since Quick and I haven't gone on what would be construed as a date in a long time. Keaton Jeffries was more on the mark when he sniped that I was banging one, not knowing how spot on he was. "But I don't know much. Just that there was a threat against the school, against some students and some staff members, and until they know if it's credible or not, security is going to be tightened. That's why there are more guards around; that's why things are going to be searched more thoroughly."

A voice behind us makes both of us jump. "Ladies," Keaton says as he slithers past us. That voice would make me jump under any circumstances. My mind races as I debate whether or not to tell Freddie about the drawing I did of Sachi's rapist that looked an awful lot like him. She dated him, I think with a shudder. She should know.

Principal Wimbish's office is shuttered and dark. I frown. "Shouldn't she be here?"

"She probably is," Freddie whispers. "Probably under her desk with her head up her ass."

"Have you seen Violet?"

"Is she involved?"

"I don't know," I lick my lips. "I don't know what to think."

I watch Keaton walking down the hall and wait until he turns the corner before taking Freddie aside. "There's something I do have to talk with you about but not here. Are you free later?"

Freddie hesitates, like she's still debating whether I'm on the level and that transparent doubt sears me. "I'm busy tonight, but coffee after school sounds good. It would have to be closer to four-thirty. And not too far from here."

I nod. "Good." I want to redeem myself in her eyes and it's not like we didn't already suspect Keaton of being a sleaze. I know full well Quick wasn't completely sold on my drawing, insinuating that my personal prejudice against Keaton influenced me, but I only drew what Sachi described. If I didn't know Keaton, if I didn't hate his guts, would the drawing have come out the same way? I haven't once smelled any cologne on him, much less the asphyxiating one that whoever assaulted Sachi was wearing, the cologne I smelled on the subway platform before Ripley Herrera was crushed by a Brooklyn-bound D train. Having seen Keaton in action, hitting on the ladies when we were out for drinks only a couple of nights ago, it's not hard to imagine a drunk Sachi was an easy mark.

But was it rape? The ABC task force is still looking for someone quite different; Quick told me as much but not much else. Sachi's case is an isolated incident as far as they're concerned, an anomaly. The case of Deidre Marx, the murdered substitute teacher, less so, though she dated Keaton too.

The bell jars me into the present. The girls practically follow me into the classroom, toting their twice-examined backpacks and even more attitude than usual. Julissa slams her backpack on her desk and announces, "I'm not in the mood to draw today."

"Fine, fine," I say. "You can do whatever you want."

"I want to go home, Miss P," she snaps, "so that crazy-ass purple-haired bitch doesn't pop me off."

I don't have to ask who or what she's talking about. The other girls take their storyboards out of their bags and busy themselves with sharpening pencils and culling through more magazines for images they want to use. Aubrey shrieks and makes the other girls jump. "This!" she holds up a picture of a cartoon character with purple hair. I almost can't blame Violet for having a vendetta, if that's what she has. I clear my throat and ask, "Has anyone seen Violet?"

Julissa shrugs nervously and shuffles her feet under her desk. Aubrey clears her throat. The other girls shuffle in their chairs like they have an itch they're too embarrassed to scratch. I take a deep breath and press on. "Does anyone have any idea where she might be or who she might be with?"

"Her boo," Julissa says. "Yeah, even someone like Violet has a boo. And I don't."

"Hot boo too," Aubrey mutters.

"Who is he?"

"Don't know his name. It's not like we've been formally introduced," Julissa snickers. "I've just seen him. Seen him practically giving her a tonsillectomy. He was a friend of Ripley's. I saw him with her a couple of times."

"Ripley...the girl who..." I don't want to rehash that tragedy. "Does he have a car?"

"I've never seen a car but he meets her after school sometimes," Aubrey pipes in.

Another girl, Darlene, raises her hand to get my attention. "I saw her get in a car with him yesterday."

"You did? Was it her boy, er, boo?"

Darlene nods. "He was wearing a hoodie hiding his face, but it was him all right."

"And you're sure?"

"No doubt. He's a hot boo." Darlene looks down at her storyboard and the other girls look at me as if they're practically begging, *Can we drop this line of questioning please*?

"Okay, let's get to work," I say, hoping that if they think of something connected with Violet's disappearance, they'll let me know. It doesn't seem like they miss her much, so maybe they won't. But at least I got this out of them. Not that it's much. But if Violet's "boo" drives legally, he's at least eighteen and she's probably at most fourteen. Were those his hands she drew? I didn't get that picture.

Where is she and what's her story and where is her storyboard?

Suddenly a shriek blasts through the PA system, repeating in bursts of three, sounding like a swarm of angry birds. "Fire drill!" one of the girls in the back of the room shouts, grabbing her backpack. The other girls scramble to their feet and make a dash toward the door only to be confronted by a guard at the door. "Shelter in place," she commands.

I'm halfway out the door when she backs me up. "Lockdown," she says. "Lights out, lock the door, everybody down, you know the drill."

Apparently the girls do. They drop their backpacks and crouch beside their desks, away from the window. I follow suit, wondering whether the principal is in fact under her desk, too, or whether her head is up her ass as Freddie suggested or not. *Where's Freddie?*

"I wish I had my fucking phone," Julissa snipes. She has a point. I have mine and I feel guilty that I can pull it out if I want to. The phones are doing the girls no good at all checked in at the truck in an emergency. I can hear sirens and voices outside and then louder voices in the corridor. "I don't feel so good," Aubrey announces. She doesn't look so good either. Maybe she wasn't lying when she said she was diabetic.

"No energy bars?" I ask her.

She shakes her head. "Need to go to the bathroom."

"Aubrey, you can't leave the room; we're in lockdown."

Her immediate response is to throw up next to her desk, eliciting groans of disgust. I scrounge through the desk drawers looking for something, anything to wipe up the floor. The girls may have had to check in their phones but I still have mine on me and it could be a matter of life and death. Or maybe not, but I need to be in the loop. I call Quick's cell number and expect it to go directly to voice mail, but he answers on the second ring. "What's going on out there?" I ask, my voice quavering. "We're in lockdown and I have a sick student who needs medical assistance."

"How bad is she?"

I look up, catching Aubrey mid-bubble. She snaps her gum with renewed fervor. Maybe she was lying when she said she was diabetic. "I'm not sure," I say. Maybe it was just nerves. *I hope it was just nerves.* "What's going on out there? Was anyone hurt? Are any students out there?" I'm only thinking of one.

"We've secured the area. Doing a sweep. Nothing so far. We're looking for a male, roughly seventeen to twenty-two years old, six feet tall, light complexion. There's reason to believe he's a person of interest behind this. Stay where you are and away from the windows."

Violet's "boo," maybe? Who is he and what could he have to do with this? I debate whether I should go back to asking the girls more questions. Did you see him and Violet anywhere else? Someplace where he might live? Is there anything that could make him want to threaten the school? *Like the way you treat Violet?*

"We may be here a while," I say to them. "Why don't we go to the back of the room and sit on the floor and work on your projects." I'm not sure how much work they'll get done. I want nothing more than to peek out the window and see for myself what's going on. I hear a pop outside, then another, then another, and change my mind. I may be sick to my stomach myself. More sirens wail in the distance. The whir of what I think must be a helicopter joins the chaos chorus. The girls are looking at me, seeking answers I can't give them. A couple of them make half-hearted attempts at drawing and then stop. The ring of my cell phone makes me jump. I tap the answer icon. "It's over," Quick says.

"What happened?"

"The situation is under control. It's over. Is everyone all right in there?"

"In this room, yes," I say. "What about...what happened out there? Was somebody shot?" I put my hand out as if I'm trying to calm the girls, but I'm mostly trying to calm myself. I hear activity in the corridor, finally, various shuffling footsteps and then the staccato click-click of impossibly high stiletto heels. Maybe Freddie knows more than I do. Quick isn't giving up anything. "I'll call you later," is all he says. *It's over, glad you're alive, there's nothing I can tell you.*

"You can go back to your seats," I say. "And wait until the bell dismisses us." I open the door a crack and slither through. "Freddie!"

Freddie wheels around. I see uncertainty in her face again. I'm not sure how I can convince her that my relationship with Quick has nothing to do with all of this and that I'm not working for him or with him in any professional way. I'm not even sure if I can call it a relationship right now or if I want it to be or how I can make things be right. *Maybe nothing will ever be right.* She points down to the floor, to a trail of red dots getting somewhat bigger until they are as big as blotches, leading us down a few doorways to the nurse's office. "I can hear Keaton even before seeing him."

"What do I have to do to just get a fucking bandage?"

The nurse looks like she could tend to a cell block at Riker's Island but still seems like no match for Keaton in his frenzy. "Give me paper towels, a rag, a sanitary pad, something!" Blood is seeping through his fingers. The security guard at the front door mumbles something into her two-way, relieving me of having to call Quick back, right in front of everybody.

"You've got to apply pressure to slow the bleeding," the nurse says, looking like she could and would like to apply maximum pressure if so needed. Keaton jumps like he was seared with a hot iron. "Don't touch me," he shouts. "I'll do it myself."

"Looks like somebody went too close to the window," Freddie says. "Glass must have shattered on him. Douche."

I frown. If it were a matter of only the window shattering, wouldn't his sleeve have protected his forearm? "I think he was shot," I whisper. "I heard pops...coming from out there and his room faces out the same direction as mine."

"Too bad it wasn't a little lower," Freddie says.

"You don't know the half of it."

Freddie raises an eyebrow. "Was your room shot at?"

"No, no, no broken glass. I think I would've noticed. Maybe I wouldn't have noticed." My mouth is so dry I can barely talk. "I really better get back to my class."

Static that sounds like the mechanical version of throat clearing bursts through the intercom near the ceiling. "Attention, students, faculty and staff, due to unexpected circumstances, school will be dismissed early. Please return to your home rooms for final attendance and instructions before dismissal."

A couple of uniformed cops brush past the metal detector and head to the nurse's office to transport Keaton, who is still resisting. "I don't want to go to the fucking hospital," he bellows.

"Nobody asked you if you wanted to," one of the cops says, herding him toward the door. I have to hope the exam they give him is more than just physical. I want to get away from this.

I take a deep breath. "Can we still meet later?"

Freddie nods. "Should be even easier now. Still, not until four-thirty."

"That'll work," I say. "There's something I have to do first."

24

D r. Zimmerman's office is exactly how I pictured it; "psychiatrist modern" would best describe it, at least his waiting room, which is as far as it seems his receptionist will let me advance. At least she can't hang up on me like she did three times before I decided to just show up. "The doctor is extremely busy. He can't take walk-ins," she snaps.

"I'm an emergency case," I offer. I'm still shaking from the lockdown at the school; it's not a lie.

"Did you consider going to the hospital?" she says.

"This was closer."

"Dr. Zimmerman can't possibly see you today. He has appointments until five."

"I'll wait."

"After which he sees patients at the hospital, so maybe he'd have seen you if you went there." This woman is enough to drive borderline patients to a padded cell. "And you're not even a regular patient of his."

"Sometimes it just takes a crisis," I say. I'm wondering if I should start telling psychiatrist jokes, laugh inappropriately or maybe start breaking things. "I'm a teacher at GreenWood Middle School. There was a shooting there this morning..."

The door behind the reception desk opens and a man not much taller than me peers out. He's nothing like what

I pictured, even with Freddie's sparse description of him. He's graying around the edges and attractive in a rough way. I could picture him shooting darts in the bar Freddie and I visited more readily than resolving troubled patients' angst. And I have considerable angst right now. I really should have gotten a waitressing job. I wouldn't be agonizing over these girls I have no control over, these girls careening toward scary lives. *I wouldn't be ducking bullets.* I still have no idea exactly what happened outside and my calls to Quick have gone straight to voicemail. So when Dr. Zimmerman signals me to come in his office, I look at it as maybe a way to get some additional information about Violet as well as an opportunity to vent.

"I don't have much time," he says.

"This won't take much time," I sit down without being told to, on a chair rather than the proverbial couch. The air in the office is stifling even with a window air conditioner unit humming loudly in the corner. When he comes closer, walking past me to get to his desk, I get a whiff of cologne. *The same cologne I smelled in Sachi's apartment.* The smell makes my eyes smart. "I was at a school where there was a lockdown this morning...someone was shot...I'm very traumatized." I neglect to add that the person who was shot is on my shit list. "I never thought I'd be teaching or putting myself in a position to worry about other people so much." I look up from scrunching a tissue into a ball in my hands to see if he's taking it all in. "I understand you saw some of the girls as patients, before this, did any of them strike you as someone who would do this?"

"That would be privileged information, Miss...."

"Price. Delilah Price."

"I could no more tell you about any other patient's mental state than I would tell someone on the school staff that your emotional state might make you unfit to teach.

In general, no, no one stands out to me as someone who would carry out a threat."

"Does that mean they made a threat?"

Dr. Zimmerman blinks. "I didn't say that."

"One of the girls is missing...she's a cutter and I'm worried about her. She left school yesterday and no one's seen her since and I wonder if she poses a danger...to herself."

He flexes his fingers back and forth. If he wanted to distract me, he did but not in a good way. He has big man hands. Of course it would help to see Violet's drawing again to compare, but I have no idea where her drawing might be. Or where she might be. I feel a frisson of fear as I look into his unreadable eyes, as his fingers flex back and forth and I smell that asphyxiating cologne. It's certainly not like he's the only person who wears that cologne, whatever it is, but I've never smelled it on Keaton and he's the person Sachi described yesterday. Or was he? I'm not sure whether I can trust Sachi's account of anything any more. I'm not sure if I trust my own judgment. Self-doubt sucks. Maybe I belong in a psychiatrist's office.

Just probably not this psychiatrist.

"I can't talk about any patients, Miss Price."

"Is Violet Velez one of your patients? Or Julissa Dias?" I go for broke. "How about Ripley Herrera?"

Dr. Zimmerman's lips tighten. "I thought you were here because of your anxiety? It's obvious you're very upset. I can give you something for that."

"I don't want anything for that. I want answers."

"Maybe you should be asking the police to find this girl." He reaches for my hand as if to calm me. "You're having an anxiety attack." His fingers reach for my hand and I pull away. His touch makes me want to scrub up. I bolt out of the chair and head for the door.

"You're damn right I'm having an anxiety attack!" I shout.

"Let's talk about it," he says. The corners of his eyes seem to be twitching. *Who's anxious now?*

I don't trust him to merely talk. He seems all too eager to prescribe something and I'm afraid of what that something might be. I rush past the receptionist desk and out the door and hurry down the dimly lit stairwell, eager to reach the door and find refuge on the street. Suddenly I feel a thud on the back of my head and my knees cave from under me. A hand grabs at my messenger bag and yanks it from my shoulder. Oh great, I'm being mugged, I think, feeling like all the action is taking place slow motion at some distance away from me, that I'm just a passive witness, except for the pain. My head throbs and my lungs fill with the scent of overwhelming cologne, the same cologne I just smelled upstairs. Either Dr. Zimmerman followed me down here or that scent is a best seller among miscreants. I scramble to my knees just as I'm grabbed from behind again and feel my arm being swabbed with something. I twist and jerk my arm free just as the front door to the building opens and an old woman teeters in carrying a bag of groceries. I stagger past her and turn to look behind me only when I feel it's safe, with the door wide open. Nobody is behind me now. How did I not hear him coming or going? All of my belongings seem to be here, though, scattered across the faded Oriental rug. I sink to my knees again to start picking them up and manage only to cup my phone in my hand. I'm relieved I thought to add a favorite contacts app so I can dial Quick with one tap of my shaking finger.

25

"What happened, Delilah?" Quick looks me up and down, not the first time I've been looked up and down since I arrived at the ER, or at least the hallway leading to the ER, and I want nothing more than to get out of here. It occurs to me that I never did call Freddie. It's not like I intentionally blew her off; I was semi-conscious at the time. My head still hurts, but luckily nothing is broken. Except for maybe my spirit. The paper gown I was talked into wearing is hospital issue and not very flattering and doesn't hide the bruises on my arms and legs. That's not going to look very pretty when I'm modeling, I think, only I can't remember if I'm supposed to be modeling again any time soon. It's time for a back-up plan. This teaching thing isn't going so well.

"Let's just say I'm having a really, really bad day."

"Did you get a good look at who mugged you?"

I rub the back of my head. "He came up from behind, so I didn't see anything," I say. "Except it was a he." I want to wait until I'm out of here to tell Quick my suspicions about who it might be, who I strongly suspect it was. That suspect might be on staff here. "I want to go home."

"Did they say you could go home?"

"They didn't say much of anything. Too many customers and really bad service." I grimace. "Do you know I saw a rat cross the floor on my way in here? A rat in a hospital? I haven't ever even seen any near the alley where I dump my trash. I want to go home." I look down the hall and see a patient handcuffed to his gurney. "Now."

"I'll see what I can find out. Don't go anywhere."

"Where would I go?" I look down at my paper dress forlornly. "I need my clothes."

Quick walks down the hall, past the handcuffed patient who spits at him, and stops at the nursing station at the far end of the hall. It's been over an hour since I saw a nurse so I don't know how much luck he's going to have. I pull the gown more tightly around me and it makes a crinkling sound. I sigh with relief when I see him finally coming back with my messenger bag. "We're going," he says.

I gingerly slide myself off the gurney, holding my hospital gown closed as tightly as I can. "Where are my clothes?"

"Let's go," he pulls the white sheet off the gurney and hands it to me. "Use this as a toga. I'll get your clothes later. I have to come back here to question somebody."

"You're not telling me something."

"I'm not telling you a *lot* of things. Later. Let's go."

I pull the sheet around me and take a few halting steps to test my balance, then steady myself and follow him as he strides to the exit near the ambulance loading dock. I feel like the inmate breaking out of the asylum and even better, have a police escort, but I still feel like somebody's going to stop us until we make it out the double sliding doors. The heat outside hits me almost as hard as the person who mugged me, especially after a couple of hours in the meat refrigerator temperature of the hospital. Something else hits me; it's dark out. "What time is it?"

Quick looks at his watch. "Nine-twenty."

"I was in there for...nearly five hours? They barely looked at me!"

Quick ushers me to his department-issued rent-a-wreck wannabe. "I'm looking at you," he says. "Maybe we should get you looked at professionally at another hospital."

"I'll pass," I say. "Okay, we're out of there. Now can you tell me what exactly was going on?" I'm not sure if I should ask for the specifics or even if I remember what all those specifics are. My head still hurts. The car lurches out of the parking space and merges into traffic. Quick turns right, then left and eases his way into the stream of traffic on the Williamsburg Bridge. He's still not talking. *Not a good sign.* "Unless you'd rather I read it on the front page of the *Post* tomorrow..."

"There was a shooter at the school and he's on life support. Self-inflicted gunshot wound after he fired off a few rounds. One hit your buddy Keaton Jeffries. Flesh wound, he'll live," Quick shifts lanes.

"Lucky him." I shift my weight so I'm sitting more on sheet and less on worn car upholstery. "Was anyone else hit? Are the students all right?"

"As far as we've been able to determine, the only ones hit were Keaton and the shooter." Quick turns to me when he stops at a light on East Houston.

"Well, it's not like everybody loves him," I offer. I'm relieved to know nobody else was hurt. No one that they know about. But where's Violet?

Quick pulls up in front of my building and turns off the ignition with a click and comes around to open my door and offers his hand. "Can you make it?" I nod and force myself to be steady as I climb the stairs. I can see the curtains in Mrs. Davidoff's apartment upstairs part. I'll deal with Mrs. Davidoff later. Right now I'm not entirely sure how to deal with Quick. I wanted to hear from him all week and now that he's here, helping me, actually acting attentive and concerned, I may have to throw out the oldest line known to man: not tonight, dear, I have a headache. He hands me my messenger bag and I fumble inside for my keys. "You're lucky that old woman came in that building when she did," Quick says.

"Maybe luckier than you know," I say. "I'm not sure but I think whoever it was who knocked me down was trying to knock me out too. I remember he grabbed my arm and was rubbing something on it, like he was going to give me a shot of something." I frown. "I think it was Zimmerman."

"He mugged you?"

"He said he wanted to give me something for my anxiety. I bolted. I didn't hear anyone come after me but...I smelled him. Same cologne I smelled in his office. The same cologne that I smelled in Sachi's apartment, in fact, and on the Astor Place subway platform right before that girl Ripley Herrera was hit by the train."

"Popular brand."

"You think?"

Quick puts his arm around me loosely as I slowly climb the stairs, aware that I left the sheet in his car and I'm just wearing the flimsy hospital gown. I turn the key in the lock on my door and it springs open noiselessly. I close it behind us.

"Are you sure you're going to be okay?"

I nod. I feel better just by being on my own turf. I feel like the events of the last twelve hours or so have been scrambled in my head like encrypted TV signals. I'm having a hard time getting a clear picture. Quick presses against me and kisses me long and hard. His hands run along my spine, slipping them under the flimsy hospital gown, conducting a more thorough exam than the harried emergency room resident. My head may still hurt, but the rest of me doesn't, as we back up and edge to my bed. The hospital gown slides to the floor and I pull him on top of me. And then Quick's cell phone rings.

"Fuck!" I mutter.

He answers and frowns, then holds up a hand as if to say "Stay!" and paces across the room to continue the conversation. When he comes back, his face is more somber. "I told them I'd be with you all night and bring you in if you developed complications. That's how I bailed you out. But I have to go. Do you have anyone else who can stay with you?"

I immediately think of Morgan and text him. FIRE ISLAND FOR THE WEEKEND, he texts back, adding a sappy heart. I don't have the heart to tell him it's an emergency and ruin his fun. I think of Freddie, but I'm not sure what she's thinking of me right now. It's time to find out, even though my head is spinning, even though I'm not sure I can process being blown off, too, on top of everything else. Quick is right; I probably shouldn't be alone tonight. I enter her number and type out, "Had emergency. Long story. Can u come 2 my place? Will explain." Within what seems like seconds, I hear the percolating pulse announcing a reply, "Will b there as soon as I can."

"Can you stay a little while longer at least?" I finger his collar and nuzzle his neck. "Until she gets here?"

"I don't think I can do that," he says, as I nuzzle his neck and feel his tension. "I'd like to do that, but I can't." He taps his phone restlessly. I'm afraid to even ask what that call was about. Now I'm feeling tense too. "I'll try to come back later this weekend," he murmurs, leaning in for a hurried kiss, then he back steps to the door. "Let me know if you need anything." I sigh in exasperation. Barring another 911, whatever my need might be would probably go directly to voicemail.

26

"Girl, you've got some serious bed head," Freddie says at my door, playfully tousling what hasn't already been playfully tousled. She's the most dressed down I've ever seen her, wearing a snakeskin print tank and faded jeans and her usual impossibly high stilettos. I've at least put on some real clothes. "And is that a shiner you're getting?" She frowns. "What the hell happened to you? I wasn't expecting an *emergency* emergency."

"Sorry I couldn't call you earlier to get together as we planned. As you can see, I was indisposed." I launch into an account of what went down, from arriving at Dr. Zimmerman's office to being knocked down in the downstairs hallway on my way out. "And it was all for naught. I didn't find out anything about Violet. Or anyone else."

"They found a body," Freddie says.

"What? Where? Is it..." I put my hand over my mouth. I feel like I'm going to be sick.

She shrugs. "I heard snippets on the news before I left my place. I don't know if it has anything to do with this."

The way Quick dashed off without telling me anything makes me think it has everything to do with this. He would probably give some indication otherwise that it was nothing for me to worry about. It's hard not to think the worst when the worst keeps happening. "I could use a drink," I announce.

Freddie eyes me warily. "In your condition? I don't think..."

"You did a pretty good job carrying me out the other night," I remind her.

"But you didn't have a concussion."

"And I don't now. Just a bump. Come on, let's go." I feel the room sway just a little bit as I reach for my bag. Freddie shakes her head but follows me. I have to find out something, even if it's on the 10 p.m. news, even if it's on the front page of the *Post*. The heat, even at this hour, is stifling. "The hottest June on record" is living up to its billing and not in a good way. The bar I'm leading Freddie to is just a couple of short blocks from my building. Good thing.

The TVs are tuned to sports, baseball on most and playoff hockey on the others. Freddie steers me to a table near the window that has opened up and eyes the stools suspiciously. "Is this okay?"

"We'll find out soon enough," I say, hoisting my way up on one. Freddie meanders to the bar and comes back a few minutes later with a beer in one hand and a fizzy drink in the other. "Club soda," she says, sliding it in front of me. My phone rings and I hand it to Freddie when I see Quick's number pop up on the screen. "Tell him I'm sleeping," I coach her. I don't know where he is, but I certainly don't want him to know where I am and I'm afraid of what he might be calling to tell me.

Freddie frowns. "He's going to hear the noise in the background and know you're not home. Unless your place normally sounds like a bar?"

"Shit, you're right. I just won't answer then. I'll call him later," I look around. "I keep expecting someone we don't want to see."

"Oh, if it's Keaton you're worried about, he won't show up here. He has his ass in a sling. Well, actually his arm, but you know what I mean. He was going to go home after he was patched up, to visit his daddy, he said. Imagine being a daddy to that." Freddie takes a sip of beer and nearly spills it when a bulletin flashes on one of the TV screens behind the bar. Missing Girl Found Dead in Fresh Kills, bordered in blue. Then a picture flashes on the screen.

"It's not her," I sigh with relief and down my club soda in two gulps. "I could use a real drink."

"Maybe, but you're not getting one. Not tonight, anyhow."

"You're worse than a cop,"

"Oh, really? Do tell."

I laugh nervously, but the word cop made Freddie flinch. "There's not much to tell," I say. "I've been seeing him on and off for a while. Since last fall. But..." I was about to say I don't see a future with him. I'm not sure about that, but I'm not sure how he fits in my future. Or how I fit in his. Or the future, period. But one thing I do know is that I'm going to start looking for a waitressing job.

"Are you happy?" Freddie asks.

"That's a good question," I frown. "I know I'm not cut out to be a teacher. It's just something I applied to do, to make some additional money. It sucks to be a poor artist... and a bad teacher."

"But you're not a bad teacher. And I'll bet you're a great artist."

"A great *poor* artist," I finish the club soda. "I could use another drink." She reaches for my glass. "Something stronger."

"Nice try. No," she laughs as she veers through a throng watching the assorted TVs. My phone rings again. I hesitate and then answer just as Freddie brings me another club soda.

"We found that missing girl's backpack," Quick says. I'm still thinking of the one we saw on the TV and I'm just about to say it's not who I was afraid it was and wonder why he's telling me about her backpack when he adds, "Violet Velez."

"She's not..."

"We don't know," he says. "We didn't find her, not yet anyway. Just her backpack. There are recovery units searching now. I can barely hear you. Where *are* you?"

Busted.

"Freddie's with me. She'll make sure I'm okay." I look up and Freddie nods, but she doesn't look happy. What is it with her and cops? "What do you mean by recovery unit?"

"The backpack was found by the river. Look, I have to go. I'll let you know if we find her." *He always has to go.*

"Look for her drawing in her backpack. See if the drawing is there. The one with hands grabbing." I don't know if he heard me or not. My hand shakes so visibly as I put my phone in my messenger bag that it might look to the casual bar hopper like I'm having DTs.

"Recovery unit does not sound good," I say to no one in particular.

"See, you care about Violet," Freddie says, squeezing that shaking hand. "And you want to help her and if that doesn't make you a good teacher, then I don't know what does. Sorry to say it, girl, but you're hooked."

27

I've broken the cardinal rule of not listening to the news any more and find an all-news station that streams on my phone while I lie in bed, feeling better physically but dreading going to school on Monday as much as I'm guessing my students do and wonder if I should ask them to find a substitute for me, even after promising Freddie I'd stick it out until the end of the school year. Fewer than two more weeks; how bad can it be?

Pretty bad, I'm afraid.

Sleep did wonders for me and I feel better, but I wonder how long that's going to last. I shooed Freddie back home when we got back from the bar, when it was obvious I was improving, and I just slept and when I wake up, I see that it's 3 p.m. What I've found out so far is that after over a day of looking for any trace of Violet in the murky waters near where her backpack was found, the NYPD scuba unit has scaled back the search. I haven't heard from Quick since Friday night but Freddie said she'd be by and sure enough she rings my buzzer. I amble up to press the button to let her in the front door and I hear her heels click on the hardwood floor. From the sound of the door squeaking slightly open next door, so does Mrs. Davidoff. "How does pea soup sound?" she asks, proffering a bag from a deli. "And bread and iced tea."

"Very good. I promise not to act like I'm possessed."

"Huh?"

I shake my head. "And a newspaper! Let me see."

"It's not good," Freddie says solemnly. "They found a note. But they still haven't found her. And the boy they found with a self-inflicted gunshot wound? Look, here's his picture."

"Oh, crap, I didn't get a really good look at him the other day, but I think that's who Violet left with." I unfold the Daily News and wince. The headline screeches 'Dead-Wood,' a picture of the cemetery with the same name superimposed. Ouch. "That's what they're calling the school now?" I shake my head. "Mrs. Wimbish is going to love that." I can't help but feel she got her come-uppance. Too bad others had to suffer. She purposefully suppressed any bad press about the school; who knew how many students walked off like Violet did, barely noticed, or how many cries for help have gone ignored. I wonder what else she's been hiding. Maybe it's time to ask, I think; what can she do, *fire me*?

"I wonder if they found her storyboard?" I muse as I scan through the news story about the police press conference and the grandmother pleading for Violet to come home, though the note found saying she "couldn't take no more" seemed to give little hope of that.

"They probably have no clue about the storyboard," Freddie says. "Did you talk to your boyfriend?" There's a definite rise in her tone when she says boyfriend.

"Freddie," I put the paper down to look up at her. "Why do you hate cops?" My directness takes her aback; I can see that in her face. I've given her no room to deny or wiggle out of it.

"I had a brother...have a brother...when he was nineteen, he went to the neighborhood bodega to buy some things for our mom. Bumped into some of his friends on the way and they went together. The store owner didn't take kindly to them 'shopping while black' and accused Ricardo of swiping stuff. His friends...well, they might have, but not Rick. Police came and he wouldn't let them search him; they exchanged words and he tried to leave and then one of them put him in a chokehold..." Freddie's voice trailed off.

"Did he..."

"No, he didn't kill him," she says softly. "But blood flow to his brain was blocked long enough to cause ischemia that became rather permanent." Freddie lowers her head. "He doesn't even know us any more."

"Oh, Freddie, I'm so sorry." I can picture a couple of the cops I've met since last fall using a chokehold all too easily but not Quick, and I don't want to imagine Quick ever doing that. "When was this?"

"Ten years ago," she says. "Look...I don't mean to insinuate that your friend..." There's that edge in her voice again. "It just never goes away, Delilah. It never goes away."

I can't imagine that it ever would. I hand Freddie a tissue.

"Well, you asked," she says sheepishly.

"Yes, yes, I did," I nod. Now that it's out in the open, it can't be stuffed back into hiding like a jack in the box. I give Freddie a few minutes to regain her composure. I go back to the news story about the search for Violet, which doesn't tell me anything I really want to know. Whose hands was she running from? I remember chillingly her words to me when I asked her if everything was okay. *It will be.* Only it isn't. I have a lot of questions I want to ask Quick, when I get the chance. And a lot of questions for my students. I just don't know if I'll get answers from any of them. But I'm going to have to try harder and dig deeper. And I'm going to have to try not to get assaulted again in the process.

28

If GreenWood looked like a carefully guarded vault Friday, it looks like Fort Knox when I approach it after the somewhat extended weekend; police are everywhere. There are security guards, too, carefully monitoring cell phone check-ins and the line-up to go through the metal detector, I grimace as I lift the flap of my messenger bag and get waved through. The girls storm in, much like class-five hurricanes ready to raise havoc. "Are you going to strip search us?" I don't have to turn around to know that challenge is coming from Julissa. I hear a series of high-pitched beeps and freeze.

"Take your keys out of your bags and put them on the counter, ladies. We'll get this done much faster if you do. Anything you think might make this go off, put it out where we can see it."

"We'd be a lot safer if we could have our phones with us. Everyone else in the city can have them now. What if we get shot at and can't call our parents?"

"Take it up with Mrs. Wimbish," the guard says. "Her school, her rules."

I hear a clatter of metal being emptied and dumped on the table. Julissa dashes by me, swinging her backpack, and then slows up. "Hi, Miss P," she says, her expression sobering. I'm guessing that the foundation I put on my face didn't quite cover the bruises near my eye. She beats me to the classroom and holds the door open. I'm kidding myself if I think her geniality is going to last. The other girls file in, also looking at my eye. I feel like I might as well have painted a target on it. I stare at Violet's empty desk.

"Before we get to work, does anyone have any questions about what happened here Friday?" I ask, thinking, *I sure do.*

Julissa shuffles her feet. "Violet's boo wanted to kill us," she says.

"Really? Why? Why would he want to do that?" Julissa diverts her gaze to her own storyboard. I hear scraping of metal desk chairs against the floor. I wonder if she feels guilty for having bullied Violet or even acknowledges to herself that she did. The other girls nod like marionettes. They clearly think that Violet's boyfriend had it in for them, but don't seem any more ready to accept some responsibility. Truth is he didn't shoot anywhere near this classroom and Violet would surely have told him where her tormentors sat in class if they were in on it together. The only room that had windows shot out was the one Keaton Jeffries was in. Maybe he just had a lousy sense of direction. Maybe he lost his nerve and fired wildly. Maybe he wanted to shoot Keaton. He certainly wouldn't be the only one. My mind races with all sorts of possibilities. Aubrey comes in the room late, breathless, and scurries to her desk, aware immediately of the tension in the air. "Sorry I'm late," she says. "I forgot my insulin shot."

"Okay. Okay, girls, let's get busy," I push in my chair, watching them sharpen pencils and take out erasers, at least momentarily seeming cowed. I hope that events of the last few days have made them think about how they treat people. No mention has even been made of Violet, just her "boo," which isn't the most hopeful of signs. I resolve to do something I haven't done up to now, except accidentally with Violet. I begin to walk around the room to see what they're producing, though I'm not sure what to expect any more. A couple have made good use of their mixed media, depicting themselves as stars in their own orbit, surrounded by photos of supposed family members. One is strolling down what is her apparent street on one side of the board and past the White House on the side depicting how she sees herself. Lofty ambitions. Then I come to Julissa's desk and I feel a wave of nausea building. Her board has her kneeling, seemingly servicing a faceless man who has a knife to her throat. The second side shows her hand wielding her verboten Swiss Army knife. Written underneath in bold black marker is GURL POWER. She and Violet may have more in common than she'd ever like to admit. They just have different ways of dealing with it. *Maybe.*

She's only fourteen. Fourteen going on thirty. Julissa sees me looking but unlike Violet, she makes no effort to hide what she's doing. Her insolent straight-on stare, challenging me to say something, is disconcerting. The bell sounding just jangles me even more. "Julissa, can you stay...a minute?" I ask her as the others file out and she starts stuffing her supplies in her backpack. "Who?" I ask her softly after everyone else has left the room. "Who's making you do this?" I swallow hard. I don't want her to feel trapped, compelled to run away, like Violet did.

"No one's making me do anything," she says defensively. GURL POWER indeed.

"Do you have that Swiss Army knife with you?" I ask, though I don't want to imagine where she'd be hiding it. She doesn't answer, no doubt sure I'd try to confiscate it like everybody else has. I lower my voice. "Just keep it with you, you got that, Julissa? You never know when you might need it."

Great, I think, now I've condoned possible murder. Her expression lightens; she was not expecting this. I have to gain her trust. Maybe she'll tell me her deep dark secret. Maybe she'll let me help her in a way I never got to help Violet. She nods and smiles slightly, acknowledging a small victory. "And if you want to talk, I'll be here." Great, I think, so much for those waitress job applications I was thinking of filling out.

Like Freddie said, I'm hooked. I watch Julissa walk to the door, pause and start to turn her head, then merge into the stampede of girls in the corridor. I take a deep breath and walk to the break room. Freddie is just finishing up brewing a pot of coffee and a woman who I recognize as Maya the grief counselor brings a cup up to the counter. She too recoils from the sight of my eye. I take a Styrofoam cup and stand behind her. I know she has talked with Julissa; I wonder how much of that conversation was privileged, like discourse with a psychiatrist, creepy or otherwise, or if Julissa ever even got personal with her. Maybe Julissa just did her drawing for shock value, not unfathomable since it *is* Julissa, but two disturbing storyboards produced by two very different girls tell a frightening story. I don't want to rat her out for having the Swiss Army knife, even though I know I could be culpable if she uses that knife and it comes to light that I knew she had it. I want to find out what's going on before she feels compelled to use it. I no sooner open my mouth to ask Maya if I can talk to her privately later than Keaton slams his way into the break room, his arm in a sling. "Maya, what a non-surprise to see you here. Have they offered you tenure yet?" He's staring at me though, a cold glare that makes me feel chills even in the upper-eighty-degree heat.

Freddie's jaw drops. "Seems to me it should be your balls in a sling, Keaton," she snaps.

"Well, thank you for your concern for my welfare, Frederica," he replies snidely, pushing past Maya and me to fill his own cup of coffee, though there is plenty of room to go around us. He hip bumps me, still staring, and I cringe, willing him to go away. He eases himself into a chair and takes a sip, never stopping staring. Maya takes her cup with her and heads for the door. I follow her, glancing back at Freddie, having no doubt that she can hold her own; she's wearing her snake print Louboutins today.

"I think Mercury was in retrograde when he was hatched," I say to Maya in the corridor, glancing back to make sure no one can hear us. "My students... well, a couple of my students have created disturbing projects in my class," I whisper. "I know at least one of them has talked with you and..."

"Let's go in here," Maya says as she ushers me into the empty nurse's office; her cubicle is directly across from the door, separated by a curtain. "You look like you had a run-in with a bear."

"And the bear won," I sigh. "Have any of the girls discussed things that are bothering them...that aren't directly related to Ripley Herrera's death? Family troubles? Abuse?" I clear my throat.

Maya frowns. "A lot of these girls are troubled, but not all that willing to talk about what's bothering them. I'm only here to help them if they want to talk about what happened to Ripley. I know a couple of them have gone or do go to a psychiatrist but I'm not in a position to divulge..."

"Dr. Zimmerman."

"Administration made the recommendation and some of their families agreed to it, especially since it was covered by Medicaid. Yes, Zimmerman and a couple of others who take Medicaid patients."

"Was Ripley Herrera one of the girls?"

"I have no way of knowing."

"Violet Velez? Julissa Dias? Who would know? Aside from the shrinks themselves?"

"They won't talk to you."

"I know that all too well," I sigh.

"Why do you ask, if you don't mind my asking?"

"I think they're being sexually abused. Their art projects strongly suggest abuse of some kind, and in one case overt sexual abuse. It may be something they don't feel comfortable talking about, but they drew it."

"And I take it two of those girls were Violet and Julissa?"

I realize I let the cat out of the carrier. "They didn't say anything about it to me," I say. "But the drawings are disturbing and now one of them is missing."

"Sounds to me like you need to talk it out as much as they do."

"I guess," I sigh.

Maya puts a hand on my shoulder. She definitely is comforting and I don't suspect her of covering anything up, but it seems she knows not much more than I do. If only I felt the same way about those in administration. "I have to go to a meeting now, but if you want to talk further, here's my card."

I take it and slide it in my pocket as I walk back to the break room, which is empty now. I wonder if there are yet more drawings to come depicting similar horrors and resolve to take an even closer look while school is still in session. What do Julissa and Violet have in common aside from the lurid theme of their artwork? They hated each other. Maybe it's time for a good old-fashioned parent-teacher conference. I'm not sure how I can pull that off with Julissa's family without showing up unannounced at their door and if I did that, I could probably kiss any hope of cooperation from Julissa goodbye as well as my job. At least Violet's family wants answers; they might be more approachable. That might be the better place to start. And safer.

Yes, it's horrible that I was mugged leaving Zimmerman's office, but that doesn't mean he had anything to do with it, according to Quick, though he promised he would be "looking into it." And as for thinking he was trying to give me some kind of shot, I was hit in the head, right? What kind of doctor would do that and flee the minute that old woman came in the hallway, an old woman who unfortunately turned out to have macular degeneration and could barely see a thing. *A very shady doctor.* I hope Quick *is* looking into it. It's time I insist on him looking into it if he's not. And maybe have him find out from the Office of Children and Family Services if any child abuse charges have ever been filed against any members of the Dias or Velez families. And I haven't exactly forgotten about the drawing I did of Sachi's presumed attacker and how much it resembled Keaton. Just because I hate him doesn't mean he's not guilty and he's teaching girls who have acted terrified of him. I feel like I'm drowning in a pool of suspects. Meanwhile Mrs. Wimbish is hiding behind her principal's desk, as guilty as any junta leader who plays dumb about atrocities committed during their regime in order to cling to power. I think it's time for her to be confronted by rebel forces.

29

"**M**iss Price, what do you want?"

"Just a few minutes," I promise, fighting back a wave of reflux, trying to remember what I was so determined to say to her as I strutted from the break room to the office. I close the door behind me and she remains sitting behind the desk, scribbling something illegibly on yellow legal paper, then she looks up with an expression that seems to scream out, *You're still here?* "I think somebody is abusing some of the girls," I tell her, scrutinizing her face for a reaction. I don't see one.

"Based on what, Miss Price?"

"Certain drawings..." I think of Violet's depiction of hands reaching for her and Julissa's graphic revenge drawing and don't want to get too specific.

"The grabbing hands. Yes, you told me about that. Violet wanted attention and would probably be only too happy if a boy's hands were grabbing for her. She left with a boy, didn't she?"

"These were *man* hands, ma'am," I say. "Big man hands."

"And you're an expert on *man hands*, Miss Price?"

I feel a sour taste in my mouth. "Mrs. Wimbish, Violet's not the only one who's drawn pictures that suggest some kind of abuse. They're either consciously or subconsciously asking for help..."

"Most of them already go to a psychiatrist. They don't need another one."

Yes they do, if their psychiatrist is Dr. Zimmerman.

"If the girls are drawing things that are inappropriate, maybe detention would be more in order," Mrs. Wimbish snaps and I feel like I've been punched again. "You're reading too much into this. You forget you're dealing with a bunch of manipulative juveniles. The girls are playing you, Miss Price. They want you to think more is going on than actually is. Tell one of them 'no' or put them in detention and they start accusing us of wrongdoing."

"Who puts them in detention? You or a teacher?" I glower. "What are they put in detention for? How often? What does it consist of?"

"Miss Price, I've had just about enough." I wonder if she's going to put me in detention.

"Where do they go for detention? Who's with them?"

"Miss Price," Wimbish stands and looks like she could have played center for the Liberty at one time. She could stuff any one of those girls through a basketball hoop. And probably me. "You might want to know that we're actively looking for a substitute to replace you."

"Because I'm concerned about the girls' welfare and want to protect them from a bad situation."

"Because you're nosy and ask questions that are none of your business." Wimbish looks down at me with disdain. "You're a substitute. Maybe your time would be better served going back to doing whatever it is you normally do."

I think of how much I've toyed with the idea of not coming back to this job for the last week and entertained the ideas of waitressing or bartending instead. I thought of nothing but that, how I've felt I'm a lousy teacher and the girls weren't getting anything out of their classroom experience, until I saw Violet's drawing and now the one Julissa did. A student could be raped on the auditorium stage and Mrs. Wimbish would probably not do anything if it meant keeping the school open and saving her ass. I intend to do something. I'm just not sure what yet. It would be a lot harder if I lose this job. Two more weeks left in the school year, just two; I have to argue for that time without saying why I want it.

"I really need this job," I plead, biting my lip, feeling nauseated that I feel like I have to grovel for it. I need the money to pay the rent on my sublet and for art supplies, yes, but I need to find out what's going on.

"You should have thought about that before," Wimbish snaps. "We'll still expect you to come in, but you'll be notified if we find a replacement for you. Lots of others need teaching jobs too. Is there anything else?" Her look tells me there better not be.

"Um...no, ma'am," I say, backing up and letting myself out. The bell makes me jump but as in a boxing match, it signals to me it's time for another round.

30

Three days of searching the water along the East River near where Violet's backpack was found turned up nothing, and flyers posted to poles and trees and buildings haven't elicited many tips, according to the Daily News update, shoved on page 9. The black and white picture of Violet makes her look much younger and the purple streaks in her hair are indistinguishable. I mouth the words as I read them, "Velez was last seen leaving GreenWood Middle School with Desi Zapata, who is on life support following a self-inflicted gunshot wound. Zapata allegedly fired four rounds into a schoolroom window, wounding social studies instructor Keaton Jeffries." I lick my lips. "Poses a possible danger to herself and others. If anyone sees Velez, contact 1-800-577-TIPS."

I pay for the paper and start to stash it in my messenger bag so I can read more when I get home when I feel a firm grip on my wrist. A cry catches in my throat. The sight of Quick in front of me immediately puts me at ease. At least he evidently got my voicemail message that I left him when I left the school grounds. The look on his face though tells me he has news that may not have hit the papers yet and it's not good. "Over here," he gestures to follow him to the junker car. "You got fired?"

"I'm on borrowed time," I say. "Wimbish is looking for a replacement for my sorry ass as we speak. Because, you know, God forbid anyone question what's going on there,

140

why the girls are drawing lurid pictures, why an honor student would jump in front of a train..."

"The plot thickens," he says, his voice barely above a whisper. "The preliminary autopsy report on Ripley Herrera shows she was pregnant."

"Oh..." I gasp. Aside from having been in the subway station when she landed on the tracks, I didn't know Ripley, but from what I pieced together from the accounts of others, she was a hair's breadth away from being an outright goody-goody. She was mischievous enough to gain Julissa's approval, but she never got in real trouble, got good grades, and had a devoted family who had begun looking into getting her transferred to a different school. "Do you think that's why...could the baby daddy have pushed her on the tracks?" I ask.

"We don't know what happened for sure or who the baby daddy was," Quick says. "I'll bet you're privy to a lot of girl gossip in that school. Like who's going out with whom?"

I nod. "Violet's boyfriend, or who the others say was her boyfriend, apparently hung out with Ripley before she died." I think of that skinny hooded figure who is now on life support. "But the person I saw in the subway station with his arms stretched out toward her was *not* built like him."

"I thought you didn't get a good look."

"Enough to know he wasn't built like him," I insist. "He was shorter, wider, but not heavy. Violet's boyfriend, if that's who I saw with her, was a beanpole. What I saw of him. And I didn't get that good a look at him either." I think back to that scene in the Astor Place station with a shudder. "I smelled him," I remind him.

"I smell a rat, quite frankly," he says. "We can't interview Desi Zapata. The conversation would be a bit one-sided.

We've talked with Keaton Jeffries and his alibis have mostly stood up to scrutiny."

"Mostly?"

"We're not done with him yet. We haven't been able to reach Zimmerman about the incident in the building foyer. Extended weekend vacation, apparently a death in the family."

"How very convenient," I snap. "I wonder whose?"

"Gibson is looking into whether there have been any issues with OCF and these families. She's going to want to talk with some of these girls."

"One is missing," I remind him.

"The ones who aren't," he says.

"Let me try to talk with them first. The police may spook them," I say. "Have you talked with Mrs. Wimbish? That should be a trip."

"I told you we did," he reminds me.

"But I'll bet you didn't learn anything."

"What did you learn today that made you confront her?"

"One of my other students drew a picture that almost made me sick..." I hesitate, remembering that Swiss Army knife. "It seems somebody has obviously forced her to do something she doesn't want to do. But Wimbish doesn't want to hear about it, as usual."

"Did she...your student...say what it was?"

"She *drew* what it was," I say. "And I doubt she'll share. I was hoping I'd be able to get more out of her but if they hire someone else..." I clear my throat. "Let me try at least."

Quick puts his hand on my shoulder. "Assuming they don't yet, okay, see if she'll talk to you some more."

"I'll try." I say. "But what if...?"

He puts his hand up to cut me off. "Think positive," he says. This sounds so foreign coming out of him that he might as well have said it in Urdu.

"Still no sign of Violet?" I ask.

"No," he says. "Nothing."

"Who has her backpack? Has anyone looked inside?"

"There was no drawing," Quick says. "No sketchbook either. A couple of books, a three subject notebook, ruler, triangle, an eraser," he clears his throat. "And packaged condoms."

"*Not* exactly standard school issue," I mumble. "I hope she wasn't pregnant too...none of these girls are old enough to...well, they are, but they're not, if you know what I mean. Maybe this other girl knows something about her that I can get her to tell me. Though they *hated* each other." I don't want to name names. I'm still not sure if I'll even get the chance to talk to Julissa or any of the other girls again. I can picture Mrs. Wimbish working the phone until midnight if she has to if it means getting rid of me. I have visions of maybe having to resort to stalking the phone check-in line to buy some time with them. I can imagine what Wimbish would think of that.

31

My morning trek to school has my stomach jumping. I got no call from Mrs. Wimbish or anyone else telling me not to bother coming in and I couldn't reach Freddie, so I expect to hear my fate when I walk in the door. The girls look at me as I walk past the phone check in. My eyes scan the crowd for Julissa and yes, Violet too, though I know better than to expect she'd show up like nothing ever happened. I skirt past the metal detector and walk nervously past the office, debating whether I should stop in and save myself the embarrassment of being called out in front of my students. The lights in Mrs. Wimbish's office are off, if that's any consolation. I pick up my pace and head to my classroom, still expecting that door to open and to be called back. If I'm going to find out anything here today, I better find it out fast.

"Oh, thank God you're here!" Freddie exclaims from down the hall. She walks toward me and gestures me to follow her into my room. "Wimbish was looking to replace you."

"I know. I'm amazed she didn't."

"It wasn't for lack of trying," Freddie says. "I heard her in the office. Apparently she couldn't find anybody who wanted to work here."

"I tried calling you yesterday."

"I'm sorry. I was with my brother until late," she says. "If you need anything, anything, I'll be here."

"Thanks," I say. "I didn't see Julissa outside. Have you seen her?"

"I haven't seen her yet today. But I think she was called out for something yesterday and had to do detention," Freddie says with a concerned frown. I feel like I'm going to throw up. So much for getting anything out of her if she suspects I ratted her out, but I said nothing to suggest Julissa was the one who created the suggestive drawing. Wimbish would have had to search every girl's backpack to see all of the projects, something I wouldn't put past her. I think of her Swiss Army knife and where that could land her and me, too, since I told her to keep it. When I finally see her ambling toward the room, I can feel relief cascading through me, like speed. 'Hi, Miss P," she says.

"Are you okay?"

"Why shouldn't I be?" she snaps.

"Miss Shaw told me you were in detention after school yesterday."

"Yeah, so?" she snaps gum, "I threatened to kick Aubrey's ass. Only thing I'm sorry about is that I didn't do it."

At least she didn't stab her. I feel like I'm off the hook again, but I don't know for how long. "What do you do when you're in detention?"

She uncharacteristically looks down at the floor. That's a behavior I'd expect of Violet, not Julissa, who doesn't exude shy DNA. Then she looks up at me and says succinctly, "I sit in the closet."

"What?"

"What I said," she says and turns her back to me and files into class. She threw me a crumb, though, and I have to try to put together enough crumbs to make a cake. I follow her in the room and do a visual roll call; everyone seems to be here.

So is Wimbish. I see her getting out of an unmarked car and talking with the detective through the open window. I can see sweat stains on her blouse even from here. "Let's just work on our projects," I say, wondering whether, despite Freddie's claims that no replacement was found, I'll get the immediate hook like a booed-off-the-stage vaudevillian or if Wimbish will have the decency to wait until class is over. I listen for the sound of approaching footsteps, but I don't hear any. I notice that Julissa isn't drawing, but staring at me, and again I wonder if my confronting Wimbish had anything to do with her having to serve detention. I want to ask her more questions, like I promised Quick I would. I don't want the police to question her unless they have to. Maybe my punishment for getting in over my head is drowning in paranoia and guilt. Wimbish is probably enjoying just knowing she's making me squirm.

"Aren't you going to draw, Julissa?"

"My drawing is finished, Miss P. Nothing to add."

"Do you have it with you?"

She kicks her backpack but makes no effort to retrieve it from there. I wonder how safe it is in there from the eyes of others, from hands that might want to destroy evidence if it is, in fact, evidence. "I think...I'd like to take everybody's storyboards home with me to grade today. You can have them back in a few days," I stand up, trying to muster authority. "If they're not completed, I won't take off points for that. I just want to see them and grade according to the progress you've made and you can finish them when I give them back to you. Be sure to sign them."

I have to maintain custody of their projects in case I get the boot, so maybe someone can find out what's going on and not have it swept under the rather sizable rug in Mrs. Wimbish's office. If I'm not let go, they'll just get their drawings back sooner. I'm not sure if I'll be able to smuggle them out without being questioned, but there's too big a chance I won't be able to get back in. I don't want them to suspect I may not be here though. I take a deep breath as some of the girls add some hurried last strokes to their work and get up to bring them up to me, Aubrey first. I collect one after the other, trying not to pay attention to individual drawings. That can wait. Julissa comes up last, holding the board close to her so no one else can see it, and thrusts it at me. I know what I expected to see, but what I'm looking at is a blank piece of paper. "Julissa, what the..."

"If you don't mind, Miss P, I'd like to keep what I did for my private collection."

"Yes, I do mind," I say. "Actually, you should mind because I'd have to give you an incomplete if I don't have it."

She shrugs. "Whatever."

"What are you afraid of?" I lower my voice but it's not enough; the others can still hear me. The bell finally rings and the other girls herd out of the room almost as one, like island natives dodging the ash of a volcanic eruption. I take a deep breath. "Julissa, why won't you let me help you?"

"Do you think my father being deported is going to *help* me?"

"What?"

"Never mind," Julissa starts for the door.

"Who said anything about deporting your father?" I pull on her sleeve, committing a gross breach of ethics. But no more gross than what Julissa depicted in her drawing and I'm beginning to get a clearer picture. "Is that what this is about? Did your father make you...?"

"No!" Her protest is full of indignation more than fear.

"Did someone say he would be deported if you didn't...?" I close the door behind us. "Please give me the picture, Julissa. I'll help. I'll make sure your father isn't deported."

"I don't have it." I feel like I'm going to have a heart attack in the split second before she adds, "I left it home."

"Will you give it to me? Nothing, nothing will happen to you or anyone in your family." I feel like my head is going to burst. I don't know if I should be saying these things without knowing all the circumstances, but I'm never going to get cooperation from her if I don't. My teaching career seems to be about over, so why not go out in a blaze of glory. At least maybe I'll have helped somebody. "I can come to your home," I suggest and see more apprehension. "If you don't want your family to see it, I can meet you somewhere."

She frowns. "I don't want anybody to know."

That's another thing her predator, whoever it is, is hanging over her head. "You wanted me to know or you wouldn't have drawn it," I point out gently. "You won't tell me who..."

"I'm late for my next class," she says.

"Come back after," I say. "Please."

She heads out the door and turns around like she's about to say something and then ambles down the hall. I watch until she turns the corner and wonder if I should go after her, to make sure she doesn't make a mad dash out the door like Violet did. Making her feel cornered won't help matters any. I stay put, grappling with the best way to handle this. The police would scare the crap out of her. The idea of meeting her in some godforsaken place without anyone knowing what's going down scares the crap out of me. But I have to do something.

32

"What are you going to do?" Freddie asks me in the break room.

"I don't know," I confess. "And even if I do something, I'm not sure if she'll cooperate. Something happened in detention. What do these kids do when they're put in detention?"

"Mostly sit in the room pretending to do homework and squirming until they can go home," Freddie says. "The times I've monitored."

"Who else monitors?"

Freddie frowns. "Whoever hasn't got an excuse why they can't. You know how bad some of them can be in order to get there? Well, once they're there, they're worse. It's not fun. For them or us."

"Julissa said she was sitting in the closet."

"What?"

"What room are they in?"

"It depends on who's monitoring," Freddie says. "And I left early to go visit Rick, so I don't know who...I think Mrs. Holloway was supposed to be in charge yesterday, but she left early, too, so...it might have been Keaton."

"Keaton." Just his name gives me reflux. "They would be in his room then?" I go to the door, open it and look both ways. "Where is he?"

Freddie shrugs. "Cafeteria, maybe?"

"That's his room, right?" I point across the hall. Freddie nods. "I'm going in there and take a look. I know it's a lot to ask, but would you stall him if you see him coming?"

"You know I will," she says. "You're going to owe me *big* time."

"I'll deliver big time," I promise. I approach the door across the hall and slightly to the right. It connects to a labyrinth with a door on my left and a door on my right and a narrower latched door facing me. The door on the left is locked. I turn the knob of the door on my right; the door swings open and the classroom beyond is dark and empty. Maybe I'm in the wrong room after all? I back up and flip the latch on the narrow door and push it open. All I'm looking at is a depository, shelves laden with books and atlases. Is this the closet Julissa referred to? I have to slide sideways to get between the shelves and then I see something on the floor, something white and lacy that has no business being here in the midst of dusty world history tomes. I stoop down and pick it up gingerly: a pair of girls' panties, specifically a thong. Exhibit A. I stuff them in my pocket as the door rattles behind me, rattling me. I trust Freddie to have my back, but if Keaton is determined to come in here, what's going to stop him?

A loud alarm suddenly makes me vibrate along with the door and the window, painted black behind me, clatters in its frame. Great time for a fire drill! I slide forward to the door and pull the knob. Nothing happens. I pull again, thinking the door stuck in the jamb, but it doesn't budge. I can hear the faint scurry of footsteps in the corridor, the girls being herded out the exits for what I hope is a false drill. I sniff like a dog at a hydrant, to make sure I don't smell smoke, but even if there were a fire, I'd be the last to find out and the first to perish. Freddie knows where I am, I remind myself; she wouldn't let me die. But does she even have an inkling I'm locked in here?

Breathe, I coach myself, just breathe; breathe in and out, count to ten, try the door again. Nothing. My mouth feels as dry as the books on the shelves but all of the rest of me is drenched in enough sweat to make them mildew. I wipe my palms on my skirt and try pulling the door again. It springs open, sending me hurtling backward into the dusty metal bookcase, wobbling to a stop. Keaton walks in the closet, hovering over me. "Looking for something?"

I think I already found it. I will myself not to hyperventilate. *Breathe in, breathe out.* The panties in my pocket feel like an anchor, weighing me down; Keaton's stare makes me think he can see through my clothes. I might as well be going through a TSA inspection at an airport. "I made a wrong turn," I say.

"Yes, you definitely did."

"Thanks for opening the door. I have to go..."

"You're not going anywhere." He stretches his arms out, resting his palms against the wall behind me, leaning his pelvis into me. I can feel parts of him I don't want to feel. Maybe he could use these panties! I try to press myself back to get away from him, but there's no wiggle room and the shelves start digging into the small of my back. He smirks and reaches for the light switch. I smack his hand hard and bring my knee up into his groin. He stumbles back, just the momentary pose I need to dash past him and propel myself into the valley of doors and open the first one and run through the empty classroom and out into the corridor just as the girls are coming back into the building. I can only imagine how I look. I turn to my right and Keaton is coming out of the other door, making a big show of making sure his fly is zipped and preening his hair. "Next time you have uncontrollable urges, maybe we should book a hotel," he snickers. I want to kill him.

"Oh my God..." Freddie runs up to me and grabs my arm. "Are you...?"

I nod. "I'm okay."

"He must have pulled the fire alarm," Freddie whispers. "I didn't even see him. I'm sorry."

"It might have been worth it," I say, patting my pocket in part to reassure myself that the panties are still there. If trying to molest a teacher isn't grounds for disciplinary action, I don't know what is, unless it's molesting a student. But I still can't prove anything, particularly if Julissa isn't talking. Maybe these panties can.

I have to find Julissa before she leaves for the day, before something happens to her to get her guard up again, before she can get herself into trouble again. My eyes scan the corridor for her and I finally catch sight of her turning the corner on the way back in from the fire drill. I wave her over and she hesitates but then comes in my room. I shut the door. "I have somewhere I have to be," she says.

"Not detention?" I ask nervously.

"No," she says with a half-smile.

"I won't keep you," I say. "Why don't you bring your drawing to my home. I'd escort you both ways. I just want you to know nobody will get into any trouble. " *Except for the person who deserves to be getting into a shitload of trouble.*

"I can't today," she says without explanation. She doesn't look convinced. If given the opportunity to do her project over again, I'm sure she would prefer to draw stick figures or maybe a caricature of her favorite rap singer. "Tomorrow," I say. "We can do this tomorrow, okay? I want to help you. Meanwhile here's my number, in case you need it." I hurriedly jot down the digits on a piece of loose leaf paper and fold it and hand it to her. She pockets it without looking at it. I need to work out the semantics. I'm sure that bringing a minor to my place is definitely grounds for dismissal, but I can already see my fledgling teaching career in the rear view mirror so I might as well hit the gas pedal. "It'll be okay," I reassure her, though I feel anything but convinced myself. What if she pulls a Violet and doesn't show up tomorrow? Her drawing is the bit of evidence I was counting on. The panties in my pocket might be evidence I wasn't counting on.

33

I feel like somebody's following me on my way to the precinct. Paranoia really is getting the best of me. When I turn around, all I see are the usual suspects: guys with shaved heads, a multi-colored-Mohawked female. But the feeling persists. My eyes scour the landscape, taking in the occupants of the cars driving by, the bicyclists weaving in and out of lanes illegally. I feel as wet as I would be had I swam across the river. I take a deep breath and run the last few feet to the entrance and collide with a couple of uniforms on their way out.

"A thong? Not what I'd expect a seventh grader to wear," I gingerly hold it out to Quick, whose interest seemed to immediately be piqued when I mentioned it over the phone when I got home, that and being detained in the closet by Keaton, enough so to tell me to bring it to the 'house,' though he was discouraged that I touched it. He won't touch it now, so I drop it on the table in front of Detective Gibson. Gibson scowls. "No seventh grader of mine would ever wear anything like this, but was it hers?"

"I didn't ask," I reply, wondering who else's it could be. "I didn't let on that I was in that room, that I found anything, that Keaton Jeffries cornered me. I don't know what happened to her, but I didn't want to say anything until we know something. I want her trust, so she'll hand over that drawing."

"Could you make out faces in her drawing, what you saw of it?"

I shake my head. "Nothing recognizable," I sigh.

"Family member, maybe?" Gibson suggests.

"She said no."

"A lot of them say no," she sighs.

"Keaton Jeffries raped my friend." I remind her. I would hardly refer to Sachi as a friend any more, but she did still describe him as the person who forced himself on her. "He dated Deidre Marx before she was killed. He just scared the shit out of me today. I wouldn't put anything past him. And Julissa said something about being in the closet when I asked her about detention so I wanted to see..."

"Was anyone else in detention with her? Someone who might have seen anything?"

"I don't know and I don't know if any of those girls would say anything even if they did. I don't know what he's hanging over their heads."

"Did Julissa say anyone was hanging anything over her head?" Gibson asks. I hesitate. I have visions of Julissa's father being taken away by immigration and me being responsible because I tried to help her. Do you think my father being deported is going to help me, she asked. But not saying anything won't help her either. I need promises I'm not sure I'll get.

I nod. "She alluded to something like that."

"Is it her immigration status?" I don't say anything. "If she's being threatened and can turn evidence, she and her family can qualify for a U visa. As long as no one in her family is in any legal trouble. It gets more complicated if they are but not impossible. It depends what it is. Would she be more willing to talk with us if she knows it could mean her family staying here hassle-free?"

"I would think." The relief I feel makes me almost buoyant. I can only hope it will make Julissa feel the same way. As long as there aren't fresh skeletons in her family closet that I don't know about.

Gibson gestures at the thong. "We'll run this for prints, blood, hairs, semen, DNA. You handled it, right?" I nod again and she scowls. "Looks too big for a seventh grader. But we'll see."

"What are you going to do about Keaton?" I ask. "I swear I was followed here."

"It wasn't by him. He was taken in for more questioning," Quick says. "I reached out to the Seven-Two after you left GreenWood. They're also going to toss his apartment. We're waiting on the warrant. They'll be in touch." I have a vision of his living quarters being thrown out of a high rise, which is what I'd like to do to him. "I'll be in touch," he asserts, standing up. I'm not sure if he means literally or figuratively. "I want you to go ahead and make arrangements with Julissa to bring you her drawing. I'll have a plainclothes shadow you, to make sure you're both safe."

"Was somebody shadowing me before I got here?" He frowns. "If Keaton wasn't following me, who was?"

"Did you see anyone following you?"

"I just know," I insist. "You know what they say; just because you're paranoid doesn't mean they're not out to get you." I gulp. "What about the ABC rapist? He's still out there, isn't he?" There hasn't been news about the ABC rapist, since Deidre Marx was found in Inwood Hill Park, whatever that means, but I take it to be a sore spot that he is still out there. I hear a lot of nervous paper shuffling around me. I wasn't thinking ABC when I felt like someone was following me, but with Keaton supposedly being detained, I'm not sure what to think. Maybe I really am going crazy.

"He could have gone out of town or be laid up. Or he could have been given R and R in one of our fine 'city resorts,'" Quick quips. "The task force is checking for recidivists who might have wound up in detention since his last known attack, checking prints, DNA, nothing has turned up yet."

"Maybe it's Keaton," I suggest.

"Yes, maybe," Quick says. "And maybe it's the sanitation guy who picks up garbage in the neighborhood he usually strikes in or a sales clerk in a bodega who bags his victims' groceries or a neighborhood professional who keeps regular office hours by day and prowls at night, like a werewolf. We're looking into everything, believe me."

"Be sure to look by the light of a full moon, if it's a werewolf. And load your gun with silver bullets."

The expression on Quick's face is suddenly less gentle, but he doesn't say anything. Gibson dons a pair of gloves and slips the thong into a clear evidence bag. "Call us tomorrow morning and we'll set up surveillance for you and Julissa. I'll want to see that picture myself and talk with her."

"If she won't...?"

"If the girls don't file a complaint, it would be hard if not impossible to book him for anything that would remove him from the classroom."

"Is that all? Just removal from the classroom?"

"At this point, yes, unless it turns out he's the ABC rapist. Sachiko won't file a complaint. If the girls don't, it's second period social studies as usual."

"How about if I file a complaint? He accosted me in there."

"We can get him for unlawful imprisonment," Quick agrees. "Which is a misdemeanor."

"Slap on the wrist," I grumble.

"Pretty much. Apparently he's accusing us of unlawful imprisonment."

"He would."

The phone closest to him rings and he reaches for it. After a hurried hello, his expression tells me what he is hearing is not good news and my stomach seizes up. Aside from a few "uh huhs" he's not saying anything to carry the conversation. "Thanks, Javier," he grunts and hangs up. "Desi Zapata, our shooter, just died without regaining consciousness."

My thoughts flash back to Friday, to Violet and her "boo", to Keaton holding a sanitary pad up to his bleeding arm, to my ill-fated side trip to Bed-Stuy to pay a visit to Dr. Zimmerman's office, all in dizzying sequence. And now finding out what motivated Desi to shoot at the school becomes infinitely more complicated. *Viva Zapata indeed.* Did it have to do with Violet and how would Violet react if she knew he was gone? Hard to say since it seems she's gone too. "What about his family? Do they know anything?"

"They're insisting their sweet innocent son was shot by the police. As per the lawyer who contacted us."

"Great," I shake my head. "He wasn't, was he?" Quick doesn't say anything, but his eyes look angry again. I turn to Gibson. "I'll call you tomorrow morning as soon as I have a chance to talk with Julissa." I look at Quick on my way out, but he doesn't hold my stare. My sudden questioning of authority isn't fitting him as well as his tailored shirt and his holster. My stomach feels like I overdid it at an eat-all-you-can chili cook-off, but I haven't eaten at all and now I don't want to. I just want answers.

34

While waiting for the girls to come to class, my stomach feels as bad as it did last night, maybe worse. I'm not sure how I'm going to occupy them when they get here since I collected their selfies yesterday. I didn't see Julissa on my way past the phone check in this morning. Maybe she overslept, something I so badly wanted to do. I can so relate to anyone waking up and not wanting to go to school right now. I hear footsteps in the hallway and voices taunting each other. Business as usual. Look professional, I remind myself; maintain your "gurl power," as Julissa would call it. Keep a brave front. *Hard to do when I'm not sure anymore who has my back.* Aubrey saunters in, followed by the others, ambling to their seats, looking confused about what I might expect of them. Everyone but Julissa. I get up to close the door and look both ways in the empty corridor. I should have insisted on accompanying her yesterday, no excuses. I should have had her back. *Where the hell is Julissa?*

"What are we supposed to work on?" one of the girls sitting in back of the room asks. I realize that I don't know her name. I've been teaching them two weeks now and I don't know everybody's name. Just the troublemakers and the ones in trouble. I wonder if it's that way in every school in the city or if it's just another marker of me being a lousy teacher.

"Why don't you do portraits of each other," I suggest. "With your non-dominant hand."

"What? Those will really suck!"

"It's just an exercise," I stress. *It's just something to keep you guys busy while I try to find out if we have another missing persons case.* I pause. "Has anyone seen Julissa this morning?" I ask, like I'm asking if they think it'll rain this morning, forcing a smile even, trying to keep panic out of my voice.

"Not since yesterday after school," says Aubrey.

"Did she say anything about not being here today?"

"No. Think she said she had some kind of appointment. But that was after school, not today, I think. I was supposed to go over her house last night but when I went, nobody was there and the lights were off."

"I'll be right back," I say as I head to the door, to look up and down the empty corridor again. I hear the click of heels coming closer, turning the corner, and gesture Freddie over as soon as I see her. "Have you seen Julissa?" There's no hiding my panic now. What did I set her up for?

Freddie squeezes my hand. "No, but I haven't seen Keaton yet either," she adds, as if that might reassure me. It doesn't. Last I knew, he was being questioned, but unless the detectives sent to his apartment found a dead body, I got the feeling he wasn't going to be staying long.

"She said she'd hand over her drawing to me today. After school. But now she's not here. This is too much."

Freddie gestures toward my classroom. "You can't get upset in front of them."

"I know. I know—that's why I'm in the hall." I swallow hard. "Aubrey said she had an appointment of some kind and that nobody was home when she went over there last night."

"People do go out," Freddie says, but she looks as worried as I feel.

"Julissa was afraid of her father being deported. Maybe her mother too. Maybe her, too, for all I know. I think he threatened her, to keep her quiet, and if he knows about the drawing, if he found out she let on..."

"Do you think the police would help her out there?"

"It seems they are willing to, if she cooperates," I say. "But I have to find her to be able to tell her that."

"We'll talk later," Freddie puts her hand on my shoulder. She has her class to teach and I have mine. A robot would do a better job than I feel capable of right now. The girls look up when I come back in the classroom and then go back to trying to draw each other. I hear whispering and snickering under their breath and I don't even feel compelled to call them out for it. And the last thing I want to do is look at any more of their drawings right now. I'm afraid of what else I might find out.

The bell announcing the end of class makes me think of the gong between rounds of a boxing match and I feel like I've gone twelve already. I may still not know much about hockey, Quick's favorite sport, or any other sports, but I remember sitting on the far end of the couch while my father swigged a beer as he watched boxing, wondering why anyone enjoyed watching others getting pummeled.

"Aubrey, could you wait a minute?" I ask as the girls bump into each other in their hurry out. I have no idea if they drew anything at all. Aubrey looks annoyed. I wait until everyone else has left. "Do you have any idea where Julissa might be?"

Aubrey shakes her head, but avoids looking at me. "Have you talked to her?" Again, silence. "Aubrey, if you do, please tell her I think I can help her." As I watch Aubrey amble down the hall chewing her sugar-free gum, I hope she's at least chewing on this and relays the message to Julissa if she does know where she is. I suspect she does. Just before she reaches the corner, she looks both ways and retreats. "You can really help her?"

"Yes, I can," I say, crossing my fingers behind my back. "Hiding won't help her." Her or anybody else who's been victimized, I think, but I don't want to say anything about that to Aubrey because I'm not sure what if anything Julissa told her about that.

"She said her family's going to be sent back to Colombia. Her too. I don't want her to go."

"Did she say why?"

Aubrey averts her eyes again. "Somebody reported them to the government."

"Did she say who or why?" I clear my throat. "Do you know where she is now?" Aubrey engages in a one-way staring contest with the floor.

"Aubrey?" I'm afraid she's going to claim to be on the verge of a hypoglycemic crisis again like the day of the shooting, whether real or not. "When you said you went to her place last night...did you go to where she lives or where she's staying?"

"I have another class," Aubrey says.

"Where is she, Aubrey?"

"She's not with her parents. They're hiding somewhere else. She's staying with an aunt. She wanted me to pick up homework she did for another class."

"Did she give you anything to turn in for this class?" Long shot I know, but in lieu of actually having Julissa here, maybe at least her drawing would help.

Aubrey shakes her head.

"Where is she?"

Aubrey hesitates, still obviously questioning whether she feels she can trust me or not. She sighs deeply and whips out a small spiral notebook out of her backpack and writes furiously for about a minute, then tears out the sheet of paper and hands it to me. "It's in Jackson Heights, around the corner from an Indian restaurant. I don't know the apartment number." Aubrey shrugs. "Julissa met me in the lobby."

I fold the paper and stuff it in my pocket. "It's okay, I'll find her," I say, wondering if Julissa might have given her the slip, might not even be staying in the building where she met her. I wouldn't put it past her. I'm not sure if I will find her, but I have to try.

My cell phone vibrates and I want to close the door before answering. I still feel guilty using it when the girls can't use theirs. "Thank you, Aubrey," I force a wan smile. Only when I hear her footsteps retreat in the corridor do I check my phone and see that the caller left a voicemail message. I brace myself and hit play. *When are you bringing Julissa in?"*

"Your guess is as good as mine," I tell Quick's incoming message.

35

When I get off the Seven train at Roosevelt Avenue, I feel overwhelmed by the smells of musky spices and too-floral perfumes, making me feel like I landed on a tropical island of indeterminate origin, except that there are no palm trees. I check my phone nervously; I called Quick back before I abruptly left GreenWood only to be prompted to leave a voice message, which I didn't, but I still expect him to call me back once he checks his queue. I'm still not sure what I'm going to be able to tell him until I catch up with Julissa.

As I turn the corner past a Tibetan food cart and an old man selling tchotchkes from a rickety stand, I catch a whiff of something familiar to me and not in a good way. I smelled it before in Sachi's apartment after she was raped, I smelled it on the Astor Place subway platform before Ripley Herrera fell or was pushed in front of the Six train, and I smelled it in Dr. Zimmerman's office and after I was mugged. I start to feel I'm being followed again and spin around to confront whomever it is, but I just see strangers. Did whoever it was have time to duck out of sight? I take a deep breath. It's not Keaton, I remind myself, though I've gotten no confirmation from Quick that it absolutely can't be him. Maybe I should have taken that call from him earlier. Maybe I am paranoid after all. If I cop to feeling like I'm being followed again, I'm afraid no cops will take me, or my concerns about my students, seriously.

My ringtone jars me and I pull my phone out to see who's calling, expecting it to be Quick or Gibson. I'm relieved to see my caller is Freddie. "Are you okay? Wimbish was looking for you and had a hissy fit when she couldn't find you."

"To fire my ass, probably."

"I told her you didn't feel good."

"That's not far from the truth," I nod.

"Are you okay?" she asks again, more earnestly.

"Relatively speaking..." I pause. "I'm on my way to find Julissa and get her drawing so maybe we can get to the bottom of..."

"Julissa was busted," Freddie says. "Shoplifting. Wimbish was contacted because they couldn't reach her parents."

"What?" I feel like I've been sucker punched. I don't know what I'm doing here. I don't seem to be helping anybody. I ran off to try to help Julissa and she just made matters that much worse for herself. I pass a missing person flyer with Violet's picture posted on a boarded-up window of a former travel agency. At least Julissa didn't end up like her. *Yet.* I try to take a couple of deep breaths, but the humid air gets stuck in my throat. The temperature had to have shot up twenty degrees. I lean against the concrete wall behind me for support. "Freddie, I don't know what I'm doing here. I don't feel like I'm doing anyone any good. I'm..." I gasp. "I think I'm going to be sick."

"Where are you? Stay there. Stay where you are. I'll meet you..."

"Near the elevated subway. Roosevelt and...um..." I look for the closest street sign and find myself staring at Dr. Zimmerman. I don't know what he's doing in Jackson Heights and I don't want to find out. I stuff my phone in my pocket mid-conversation and pivot and run back toward the elevated subway station, weaving around rotund abuelas carrying groceries in string bags and trying not to bump into them. I turn back only when I reach the crosswalk and see Zimmerman at a distance behind me, but heading my way. I was right. I *am* being followed. I'm not sure if it wouldn't have been better if I were just being paranoid. I feel as wet as I would be had I swam here. My white blouse is sticking to me in all the wrong places and I'm pretty sure from the way some male passers-by are looking at me that it's see-through by now. It should bother me, but I'm more bothered by Zimmerman being on my tail. If Julissa hadn't been arrested, I would have unwittingly led him right to her. If Freddie hadn't called me, I would have been there by now, walking right into who knows what. Aubrey could have even set me up. *Yes, I'm paranoid all right.* I turn around only to see Zimmerman gaining on me. Shit. I pick up my pace while looking behind me and then start to run. I dodge a rack of saris and a chubby dachshund sniffing around for a place to pee and then hit my stride again, not even bothering to look back. My foot catches on a crack in the sidewalk and I flail my arms to try to keep my balance but fly forward, landing half on the sidewalk and half in the street, my hand hitting the road, trying to break my fall.

Somebody behind me yells, "Miss, look where you're going!" It's too late for that, I think ruefully. Somebody grabs my arm and helps me to my feet and backs me up onto the sidewalk right before a cab scrapes against the curb. I'm afraid to turn around to see who it is. A small Greek chorus of spectators gathers around me, asking if I'm all right, then voicing disgust over the state of the sidewalks and the city in general. My hands sting from hitting the pavement. I'm still in fight or flight mode, but feel too wobbly to take flight and not much up to fighting either.

When I turn around, I see a uniformed officer talking on his radio behind me. I don't see Zimmerman, but that doesn't mean he can't see me. He probably ducked in someplace, watching, waiting for the Greek chorus to exit stage left. I don't have to be Cassandra to know something bad is going to happen if they do. I hear my phone ring in my pocket and pull it out. "What happened to you?" Freddie asks.

"Zimmerman was following me," I say. "I put my phone in my pocket so I could get away from him and I must have disconnected you, I'm sorry..." I gasp. "I can't catch my breath. I think I'm having a heart attack."

All I hear is dead air. "Freddie?" I don't have to look to know we've been disconnected. My battery went dead. My knees wobble. I feel like I'm going to pass out. The voices behind me sound more distant. I try to take deep breaths like I was instructed to do during post-traumatic stress counseling last year, except the air gets stuck in my throat. The policeman I saw standing to the side isn't there any more and I look to my left and right, then start to cross the street when I catch sight of Zimmerman again, right on my tail. I force my legs to move faster and weave between cars blaring their horns at me, not stopping as I start to cross the other lane. I hear a squeal of brakes and a loud thump and then metal grinding against metal. The spectators on this side of the street are acting more like disgruntled fans at Citi Field, more into blaming and shaming. "Did you see that? That girl just caused a car accident. Somebody could have got killed."

Yes, I could have gotten killed if I hadn't run into traffic. A blue-and-white pulls up to the curb followed by a very familiar beat-up unmarked car. Quick hops out and comes over to me in two swift strides. "What happened?" he asks.

"Zimmerman was following me," I say, still scanning the sidewalk for him. The increased police presence evidently discouraged him from staying around. "One of my students told me Julissa was staying with relatives near here."

"And you didn't call?"

"I did, but I didn't leave a message. I intended to call back, when I got there," I say. "But then Freddie called me and said Julissa was arrested for shoplifting and I did a one-eighty and was about to come to Manhattan when..." I shrug, still struggling to catch my breath. My knees sting and I look down at my blood-streaked legs; I look like I was in a rumble.

"Let's go get you cleaned up," Quick ushers me to his car.

I slowly sink into the passenger seat and yank the seatbelt over my shoulder. "How'd you know where I was?"

"Your friend called and said you were in distress." Quick checks his rearview mirror and pulls out into traffic, leaving me to wrap my head around this information. "Do you have any idea what you could have been walking into?"

"No, but I guess I walked away from it in time, whatever it was. I think I'm getting blood on your upholstery."

"Wouldn't be the first time. There should be a box of tissues somewhere." He gestures toward the back seat. "You also walked away from your job. I'm not sure if there's anything we can do about that this time."

"I'll wait tables," I say unconvincingly and then add, "I don't know what I'm going to do next. I don't know if I'm good at anything except sculpture and I'm not sure how good I am at it if I have to worry about supporting myself."

"Like every other artist out there?" Quick swings a right turn.

"Pretty much."

"What happened with Keaton? Did anyone find anything in his place or..."

"It stunk to high heaven. Like there was a decomposed body in there, only there wasn't. It seemed to be some kind of fruit..."

"The durian." I nod. "He was buying a durian when I met him."

"Neighbors had complained about the smell."

"That's all anybody does about him but nobody does anything about it, do they? Or have you?"

Quick looks at me askance. "He lawyered up and walked." I open my mouth to start to say something, but nothing comes out. My breath comes short and fast again. "Are you okay?"

"No, I'm not, I think I'm going to be sick..." I start to lurch forward and then the wave of nausea passes. My mouth tastes sour and parched. I lean back again and clench my jaw, hoping it'll suppress more queasiness. I turn to look at Quick, staring straight ahead as he weaves through the traffic crossing the Queensboro Bridge, reeking of determination while I'm merely reeking from sweat. He cruises down the FDR wordlessly, just occasionally glancing in my direction, and veers off the 34th Street exit. "Where are we going?" I'm afraid I already know the answer.

"Bellevue. Have you checked out," he says, turning left on Second Avenue.

The thought of sitting in the waiting room of another crowded ER makes me feel sicker than I did before, even if I do have a police escort. I swallow hard. "I'd rather not."

"You fell and feel sick to your stomach. You could have gotten a concussion," he points out.

"Just nerves, Dr. Quick." I gulp. "I'll call my therapist. The one I went to after that business last year. See what she says," When he stops for a light, he turns and stares at me and apparently my pupils aren't dilated enough to cause further alarm; he drives straight down Second

Avenue when the light turns green. "All I need is some rest to reboot," I say, trying hard not to sound like I'm convincing myself at the same time. I feel calmer on more familiar turf. I feel like the little engine that maybe could again. "I just saw Zimmerman following me and I freaked. Given that business when I went to see him. Why do you think he'd be following me unless...?"

Quick grimaces when he pulls to a stop at the next light. "We talked to his receptionist. He was in his office all day today," he says. "Booked solid."

"And you bought that?"

His eyes bore into me. "I'm not sure what I'm buying any more."

36

"I'm going crazy, aren't I?" I say it more to myself than to Dr. Patel. She hasn't said anything for a few minutes and I wonder if she wandered into a dead zone, if the call was dropped. "Dr. Patel?"

"I'm here," she reassures me in her crisp cool London accent. "And no, I don't think you're going crazy. You've been going through a lot this year and this all just brought it back. A bit of an overload, actually. If you were a computer, you'd crash. But you're not. Take a break, Delilah, I can appreciate your concern for these students, but you have to accept that you can't do more unless they come forth."

"They keep dying off," I say. "Well, one did, before I even had her as a student. Another one is missing. A third might have gone missing but got arrested instead..." I pause for breath, sensing I'm starting to hyperventilate again. "I think I lost my job today. I took off to try to find Julissa when I found out she was arrested, then I saw Dr. Zimmerman following me..."

"What...who?"

"I just told you..." Even talking about it makes my head throb again. "He's this psychiatrist my students—well, some of them—have been seeing and when I went to his office to ask him about them, he acted like he wanted to drug me and then as I was leaving, I was mugged..."

"Dr. Egon Zimmerman?"

"You know him?" I realize what a dumb question that is as soon as I spit it out. She's a therapist; of course it's possible she knows him or at least knows of him. I quickly reboot my line of questioning. "What do you know of him?"

"I did a fellowship with him years ago," she says, her voice trailing off.

I detect I've hit a nerve. "What can you tell me about him?" I clear my throat during the silence that ensues. "Dr. Patel, he was following me. I don't know why or how he's connected with all of this, but anything you can tell me could maybe help."

"It was many years ago and it's not something I feel comfortable about discussing on the phone..."

"In person, then," I say. I feel like we've switched roles and I can't explain why.

"Delilah, I have a patient," Dr. Patel says abruptly. "I can call in a prescription for you if you want."

"No, I don't want." The last thing I want is to pop a pill that would knock me out when somebody might be on my tail. "I want to talk about this."

"I'm booked solid for days," she says, sounding even more rushed and not offering a time when she might not be booked, not like the Dr. Patel who helped me late last fall at all.

"Okay, well, if you know anything about what he's capable of...if you think he could do something really criminal...contact Detective Quick or Detective Gibson at the NYPD. Please." I don't know if she's even listening any more. I click on the red end call icon, wondering, okay, *now what*? My phone almost immediately rings and for an instant I wonder if Dr. Patel is calling back to apologize, explain, offer a helping hand.

"Miss P, I mean, Miss Price, it's Julissa. I'm in trouble." I almost drop the phone. I vaguely remember giving her my number but still didn't expect her to call. *But who else would she be able to call,* I wonder? She reached out to me, now I have to convince her to reach out to the police to try to help her and I have no idea if what she just did jeopardizes the whole shebang.

"Where are you?"

"I'm in detention," she says, which reminds me that detention might actually be what led to this. "I'm in the police station. I was in a Duane Reade and I got busted for shoplifting," she says. "But I didn't."

"What did you do?" I ask. "I mean, to make them think you did?"

I hear her sigh in exasperation. "You know that Swiss Army knife?" I nod even though I know she can't see me. "I thought I was going to need it. I took it out of my bag and was holding it in my hand and store security saw me. So they said I was threatening too."

"Why did you think you'd need it, Julissa?"

"I don't want to stay here," she says, cutting me off. "This is all a stupid mistake. I didn't take nothing."

"What do you want me to do?"

"Get me out!"

"Shouldn't you be calling your parents?"

"I can't!" Her voice breaks. "Anyway I told them my aunt's going to come get me." She lowers her voice. "You get to play the part of my aunt."

"I get to what?" I clear my throat. "No, no, Julissa, there's no way I can do that. I'm sure I don't even look like her."

"Actually yes, you do, kind of. You don't know my aunt. And they wouldn't know the difference anyway because they don't know my aunt."

"Why can't your real aunt come get you?"

"I can't reach her. I've been trying...she does in-home day care so it's really weird that I can't reach her, but I want out now."

"Julissa, do you have your drawing with you?"

I hear a commotion in the background. "I have to go," she says. "Oh, yeah, I'm at Classon Avenue. Come get me."

My phone goes silent before I know Julissa ever would. I take a deep breath and call the number Gibson gave me to report if I heard from Julissa. I need back-up; I've learned this much at least. The phone rings and rings. Impatiently I disconnect and call Quick's number instead. "What's up?" he asks, sounding distracted.

"Julissa's up," I say. "She called me from where she's being held. She wants me to spring her."

"Only family can do that."

"I'm family apparently," I say. "Designated family. She apparently can't reach family."

"Where are her parents?"

"Good question. She won't say. She's still afraid they'll be deported. She apparently tried to call an aunt she was supposed to be staying with but nobody's answering and she wants out."

"Didn't you say she had relatives in Jackson Heights, where you were headed when you said you thought you were being followed?"

"I was being followed. By Zimmerman. Who was supposedly booked all day, but I know what I saw."

"What was the address? Do you have it?"

I reach in my pocket and feel the folded piece of paper Aubrey wrote it on and read it to him. I hear him inhale sharply. "What?"

"We're on the way to a possible homicide at that address," he says.

I feel like I've been punched in the stomach. "That would explain why Julissa couldn't reach her aunt..."

"We don't know who it is yet," Quick says. He doesn't have to tell me that he has a very good idea who it is. "You're not going to get her alone. I'll get Gibson to accompany you. She'll take over from there. Are you home?"

"Yes." I say.

"Don't go anywhere until she gets there."

"What do I tell Julissa?"

"Nothing yet. Have to go now."

I will myself to stay calm while I wait for Gibson, forcing all sorts of bad things out of my head, like what might have happened had I gone to the address Aubrey gave me. Quick was right; I didn't know what I could be walking into. And my footing hasn't improved any. I go to my medicine cabinet and pop open a blue tube I bought at the apothecary on Sixth Avenue last fall and let a couple of pills drop under my tongue. Just because I don't want what Dr. Patel seemed eager to prescribe doesn't mean I don't want something to calm me down. What would help me the most would be somebody who would listen. Maybe I don't need a shrink for that. Freddie would listen. Quick listens, when he has the time, which he obviously doesn't. I hear a horn tooting insistently downstairs and I sling my hobo bag over my shoulder and lock the door behind me.

37

"I'm listening," Gibson says, checking her rear view mirror as we cross the Manhattan Bridge. I realize that I've been babbling about everything that has happened in the last couple of hours, jumping from school to Jackson Heights to Julissa's phone call, but leaving out something gnawing at my mind. I know that if I told Dr. Patel something in confidence, that would be privileged information, but I'm not sure if something she told me or at least insinuated by her reaction would be accorded the same consideration. The minute I pressed her on the matter of how she knew Dr. Zimmerman, she was suddenly distant, occupied, willing only to write a prescription, so I owe nothing to her except maybe a visit from Quick or Gibson to find out what she wouldn't tell me

"I'd like to know what Dr. Zimmerman was doing in Jackson Heights when he was supposedly seeing patients in Bed-Stuy," I say. "Because it was him. It was. I saw him. Smelled him. God, I hate when men wear more cologne than women do." I clear my throat. "He was near where I was going and now Julissa's aunt turns up dead. Coincidence?"

"We don't have an ID on the vic in Jackson Heights yet," Gibson says, but her expression says it all. "So we're not saying anything to Julissa about this until we do. We need to connect her with her parents and I want you to get her to tell us where they are." Gibson pulls up in front of a red brick building that looks more like a castle than a police station, but the girl we're here to rescue is far from a princess. Gibson gestures me to follow her, turning around before we reach the door. "If there's any question about your relation to this girl, I'll get you through it. We get her out of here, then we find out where mommy and daddy are hiding."

"Easy as pie," I mutter.

Gibson stops at the desk and exchanges a few muffled words with the desk sergeant. I scan the room, thinking how remarkably similar each precinct is on the inside, almost interchangeable, the same drabness of walls and uncomfortable furniture and frowning complainants. Gibson gestures to me to follow her up a staircase to where I presume they're keeping Julissa. "They found stuff on her," Gibson whispers.

"Stuff?"

"A quarter of an ounce. Also a cologne atomizer and a Lip Smacker with the price stickers on."

I shake my head. "Was she charged with anything else?" I ask, thinking of the Swiss Army knife. Gibson appears not to have heard me as she struts down the hall to a closed door and knocks. A female who doesn't look much older than Julissa opens the door and steps aside. The minute I walk in, Julissa jumps up from the plastic chair she was sitting on and runs to me. "Tia Delilah!" If she can be persuaded to turn evidence and avoid a life of petty crime, she might have a future on Broadway; her greeting is definitely Tony worthy. I wonder if she was ever as affectionate with her real tia.

"Can we talk alone?" I ask Gibson.

"I'll be right out here," she says.

The minute I close the door, Julissa steps back from me. *Show's over.* "What happened, Julissa? I thought you said you didn't take anything?"

"It was either that or something worse," she says.

"What worse? What do you mean?"

"I took the Swiss Army knife out of my bag because I thought I was going to need it. But then I realized I was being watched and took the other stuff because then I knew security would stop me and I'd be safe until we straightened this all out."

"You took the stuff so you'd be in protective custody?"

"Something like that," she nods.

"But you still took the stuff!" I shake my head. "Who did you want to be safe from, Julissa? Who did you see?" I lower my voice to a whisper. She just glares at me. "Do you have your drawing with you?"

"It's in my backpack. They took it."

By they, I'm assuming she means the police and it's in custody here somewhere. "If you tell the police, nothing will happen to your family; you can actually do them a world of good, you can qualify for a special visa that grants them residence without worry about being deported. You took this stuff under duress—nothing will happen to you. For your friend Ripley's sake..." I know I'm really pushing it from the look on Julissa's face. "Think about what happened to Ripley and Violet..."

"Yeah, like what did happen to Shrinking Violet, Miss P? Don't even compare." The enmity in her voice is like a wake-up slap. I blew it. I decide to let Gibson take over from here. Julissa is sure to be accorded amnesty if she cooperates; what sort of amnesty from possible abuse will Violet ever see?

"Do you have any idea where Violet is?" I ask tentatively.

"Well, she's for sure not with her boo."

I open the door and gesture to Gibson to relieve me. I don't want to be in this room with Julissa right now or in the car with her going back to Manhattan. I temporarily forgot that the bullied is also a bully. I need distance from these students and this whole teaching thing and termination seems golden right now. I turn back for a second. "Whatever pushed Ripley to the edge pushed Violet to the edge and pushed you to the edge. The only way to step safely back is to stop the person who pushed you. They can't. You can. Auntie advice," I force a smile. Julissa needs a good push, but she still doesn't deserve to be abused in the manner her drawing suggested. Nobody does. "Her drawing is in her backpack," I tell Gibson, hoping Julissa wasn't lying about that. I feel like I'm relinquishing custody to somebody far more qualified. I want to run as far away as I can. Or at least run to my sculpture studio, where I haven't put in any time lately and where I can lose myself in plaster fantasy and in the process maybe find myself again. But first I need to sleep off the last twelve hours.

"You're not coming with us?"

I shake my head. "I have things to do," I say, not the least of which is reclaiming my sanity. I want to call Freddie to let her know I'm okay and to thank her for sending the police to my rescue earlier today. Freddie is the one good thing that came out of this whole teaching experience. I want to hang with her a lot more in the future. Just not at that school. I delivered Julissa to the Special Victims Division, though not exactly in the manner expected; I don't see how I'm even needed anymore. Gibson and her squad are more qualified to deal with her now and whatever happens to her in the future.

But what is going to happen to her?

I try to push that out of my mind as I board the G train heading west, gritting my teeth as I get shoved one way, then the other. *I did all I could.* I disembark at Hoyt-Schermerhorn and strut to the uptown platform, wishing I could look and feel as self-confident as Freddie in her stiletto heels. I look around me and sniff the stagnant air to make sure I don't detect a whiff of telltale cologne and then I breathe a sigh of relief. I literally hop on the A train when the doors open, eliciting stares. I can't wait to get home, take a cold shower, get some sleep and maybe get some sculpting done tomorrow. *I did all I could.* I just don't think it was enough. If the exercise I gave the girls somehow leads to justice for one of them in the long run, it would be but last I knew Keaton Jeffries was free to walk and I don't know where Dr. Zimmerman fits in any of this.

I get off the train at West 4th Street and stumble toward the exit, the events of the day catching up with me in a very big way. My head hurts again or maybe it never stopped hurting; the adrenalin rush diverted me. I hope I'm not going to be sick again. The heat doesn't help. The subway system defies the theory that heat rises. I climb up the stairs wearily and start looking around me and sniffing again. A group of teens in baggy shorts are shooting hoops on the basketball court across the street. I walk the remaining block home feeling like I'm the only person on the street. The stairs leading to my building, usually illuminated by a bare light bulb, are only lit by the flickering street lamp. Something crunches under my sneaker and I kick it aside. A sheaf of paper covers the top step like a welcome mat. I bend down and pick it up and gasp as I recognize what it is—a missing flyer with Violet's name, age, description, and reward detail as well as her picture, stained with dry carmine splotches, Pollock-style. Somebody wrote WHO'S GOING TO BE NEXT across the top in big red block letters.

38

"**D**o you think this means she's dead?" I ask Quick as he backs away from the steps while a couple of detectives from the Sixth comb the area for any more evidence.

"Right now I don't know what it means." He gestures for me to follow him to one of the blue and whites parked against the curb. "Did you see anybody coming or going right before you found this?"

"No," I sniff. "And I didn't smell anybody either."

"You touched it, right?"

I nod. "But I didn't know what it was until I saw it. It could have just as easily been a flyer from a new pizza place."

He looks up at the second floor window. The curtain flutters closed without benefit of a breeze. "Maybe the old lady saw something."

I roll my eyes. Mrs. Davidoff sees plenty but usually only when I don't want her to and I'm sure she's seen Quick leaving my apartment more than once on non-police business.

"Your niece isn't being very cooperative, by the way," he says sotto voce. I frown and then realize he's referring to Julissa." She clammed up on Gibson. "Do you want to have another go at her?" There's more than just a hint of suggestion in his tone.

"I was ready to smack her earlier," I confess. "Wanted to anyway. What happens to her now?"

"Normally I'd say detention until her case comes up if her family can't be found. But for all we know, her real aunt may have been the only family she had or could count on. If she cooperates, we can get her into a safe haven at least until her court date."

I shrug. "I'm not sure how much good it'll do." I feel embarrassed that I practically blew up at a fourteen year old, even if she acted like an unrepentant bully. "And I'm exhausted. It's been a long day."

Quick nods. "You can do it tomorrow," he says.

"Because I have no job to go to," I acknowledge. "But I'm guessing Keaton Jeffries will still be teaching social studies." The thought makes me gag.

"I've been informed he's on modified assignment," Quick says.

"Really? Doing what?"

"He's assisting in the guidance office," he says. The look on my face is probably what compels him to add, "He won't be alone with any students and will be under direct supervision."

"By whom? Mrs. Wimbish?" I shake my head. "This sounds too ludicrous to even be a lede in The Onion. Nobody in that school is safe with him there."

"We're watching him."

"I was in the school when he was being watched and he practically molested me!" I remind him. "Who knows who he's watching now? Who's going to be next? As the flyer said."

"It won't be you," Quick asserts.

I don't feel convinced. "Well, I keep coming close..." I feel like I'm about to lose it. "Why is...whoever it is...leaving crap like this on my doorstop?"

"We'll work on finding out who left this. Meanwhile try to get a good night's sleep and we'll arrange for you to talk to Julissa again tomorrow."

I force a smile. "I'd sleep a lot better if you could stay."

"So would I," he says. "I wish I could." If ever anyone could fuck me with just his eyes, he comes damn close. I feel wet. I'm not sure how much is due to being next to him or the fact that it's eighty degrees even at 8 p.m. I go up the stairs, turning back to look at him one more time but he's already retreating to his unmarked car. *Business before pleasure, always.*

My phone rings in my pocket and I retrieve it and look at the number before pressing ACCEPT. "Hey, Freddie," I say.

"Are you okay? I was trying to call you and it went right to voice mail and after this morning, I was worried..."

"I haven't checked my voice mail. I'm sorry. Today has been one hell of a day. Where do I begin?"

"I can't talk long. I'm with my brother. Why don't we meet after school tomorrow and you can fill me in?"

"I've been expelled," I point out.

"But that doesn't mean you can't meet me after school," Freddie says, mentioning the name of a café a few blocks away from GreenWood. "How's four p.m.?"

"Great," I nod enthusiastically, even though I know she can't see me. "In the meantime, Freddie, look out for Keaton; he's back at work, probably in more ways than one."

She's already ended the call. Relax, I tell myself; she's a big girl. She knows what she's dealing with. She dated him. It's not like I've never made bad dating choices in my life, far from it, but the thought of anyone I care about being in close proximity to Keaton makes me shiver, even on this eighty-degree evening.

39

I feel like one of my students would waking up on a snow day, anticipating things I can get accomplished with my unexpected freedom. Except that it's even hotter than last night and, in my case, freedom has a price; not having a job is a price I can't afford for too long. And spending the morning in the confines of yet another precinct house isn't my idea of freedom or probably anybody else's. "See if you can get her talking about this," Gibson says, handing me a clasped manila envelope.

"Does she know about the aunt?"

Gibson nods solemnly.

I take a deep breath and turn the doorknob. Julissa looks up, scowling, then goes back to picking her cuticles. A box of Kleenex sits on the table within her reach. I sit across from her, very aware that Gibson is an unseen audience. "I'm sorry about your aunt, Julissa," I say softly. "Was she your mother's sister? Shouldn't she find out about her from you and not from us? Shouldn't you tell her?"

Julissa shrugs. "If I could, maybe I would."

"You don't know where your parents are?" I scrutinize her face, which she immediately turns away from me. "Nothing will happen to them. You'll be safe."

"Like Leidy was?"

"Did anyone ever threaten you that someone in your family would be harmed if you told…about this?" I slide the crude drawing out of the manila envelope and hold it up with shaking fingers. "Did they just say they'd be deported or that something would physically happen to them?"

Julissa's lower lip quivers.

"Did anyone at school know where you were staying? Besides Aubrey, that is?"

Her eyes narrow. "That stupid bitch didn't know where I was staying from me," she snaps.

"She told me she met you there two nights ago..."

Julissa shakes her head. "No way, sister."

"This picture..." I wave it slightly. "Did this happen to you, Julissa? Did somebody make you do something you didn't want to do?" She looks away again. "Did whoever did this threaten to harm your family if you told? Julissa, look at me, please," I clear my throat. "You didn't tell and your aunt still got murdered. If you talk to us, nobody else will be hurt."

"Says you."

"I thought you trusted me. Why did you call me from the Brooklyn police station if you don't trust me?"

"I had no one else to call," she says almost in a whisper.

"You wouldn't have drawn this if you didn't want anyone to know. You had had enough. You wanted someone to make it stop, so you drew it. Am I right, Julissa?" I catch a slight nod. "Where did it happen?" I hope I'm asking all the right questions, the same questions Gibson might have tried without eliciting a response. "Did it happen during detention?" I watch her face for any clue. My mind rewinds to the reason Julissa herself gave me for winding up in detention. *I threatened to kick Aubrey's ass.* What made me buy into Aubrey's sudden interest in helping Julissa that sent me on a wild goose chase that could have landed me right at a murder scene? I hope Gibson is getting all this down. "Did it go down this way?" I grimace almost the minute I say it. "Did the person you drew here make you do what you drew here?"

She nods slightly. I'm thinking nods aren't admissible. "Did he...."

"Yes," she says. "That and more. He finger fucked me and everything."

"And...everything?"

"He didn't put it in. He did everything but put it in."

No DNA. Super. "We've discussed the what, but not the who," I pull my chair closer and level my gaze at her. "Who did these things?"

She gulps. "He told me not to say anything or..."

"I told you, nothing will happen to you or your family."

"Yeah, and it already *did*!"

"If we had known before..." I stop myself from saying something I can't be sure is true. "Your aunt's death is being investigated. Any information you can provide will help. Who would know where you were staying and how, if you didn't tell anybody? How would Aubrey know? Who would tell her?"

"I gave that address at school."

"But only administrators would see that," I say, hoping I'm right. Who knows who can see anything at GreenWood?

"I think I gave that address at the shrink's office too," she says. "But I wasn't staying with Leidy then. I didn't think..."

"The shrink?" I jump like I would if I were in a dentist's chair and the drill hit a nerve. "You mean...Dr. Zimmerman?"

"I'm hungry. Can somebody get me something to eat already? You'd think I was some fucking criminal..."

Nice job of changing the subject. I'd bet though that hardened felons would have had a square meal by now. Not to mention a lawyer. "When's the last time you ate, Julissa?"

"Yesterday, before..." Her voice trails off. I wonder if her next words would have been, "before I ripped off that pharmacy." Or tried to. According to her, she saw something in there that made her feel that getting caught shoplifting was the least of her worries.

"Okay, I'll make sure you get something to eat. Is there anything you can't eat?" She shakes her head. "I'll be right back. Don't go anywhere." I grimace again at what I just said. *Like where would she be able to go?*

I signal Gibson over to me. "She might be more cooperative if we get her something to eat," I say, drifting into Quick's predilection for using the first person plural to suggest the force behind us. Or something like that.

"We asked her if she wanted something to eat. She declined."

"I guess now she's hungry," I suggest. "I'll pay for it."

Gibson doesn't offer to take the ten dollar bill I hold out. "I'll see if I can get someone to pick up something for her. Go back in there with her. Keep pressing. We need to know where the parents are."

"And if we don't?"

"OCFS takes over."

I turn the knob and go back in the room. Julissa glares at me. "Somebody will get you something to eat," I say, hoping I turn out to be right. I sit in front of her. "Julissa, where are your parents? They won't be deported. You really need to be with them."

"I don't want them to know what I did," she says, staring at the floor. I'm not sure if she's referring to the sex acts or the shoplifting.

"It was under duress, Julissa. You were forced to do... what that person told you to do. Who was it?"

"Mr. Jeffries," she says in a whisper and I feel all the pressure that has built up in me whoosh out. I knew it, I was right. I feel like doing a victory dance except that that would be frowned upon. I can't even demonstrate the least evidence of glee.

"When did he start bothering you?" Bothering is putting it mildly.

"In February," she replies. "He made comments before, but that's when he started touching me. When I went in for detention."

"Why didn't you say anything?"

"I tried, but..."

"But what?"

"I was told nobody would believe me and it would get worse."

Did he...bother Ripley too? I ask. "Did she say anything to you about that before..."

Julissa shrugs. "I don't know. I wasn't there."

"She didn't say anything?" I sigh. "What about that boy she was seeing? Desi? Did she say anything to you about him?"

"Not much." Her eyes narrow. I feel like I'm losing her again.

"Why were you in detention? I know you had a fight with Aubrey last time but..."

"I had a few fights with Aubrey. She picked them right where he could see...." Julissa bites her lip.

"I thought you were friends," I say woodenly.

"As if," Julissa snarls.

"Okay, so you weren't friends," I try to wave that notion off like an annoying insect. "You're saying Aubrey deliberately got you into a situation that would land you in detention? Would she have any reason...aside from not being a friend?"

Julissa shrugs. "You'd have to ask her."

"I'd love to," I say. I'd love to know Aubrey's reason for trying to send me to Julissa's aunt's address too and I'm going to have to figure out a way to get to Aubrey so I can ask her who was behind that.

"Where's my food?" Julissa asks.

"Coming," I say. *It damn well better be.* I feel like the walls and time are closing in on me. "So after Mr. Jeffries did these things, he threatened you?"

"Yes, that and I got phone calls," she says. "At all weird times. I had to answer the phone fast so nobody else knew..."

"He called your home phone?"

"And my cell. Only it didn't sound like him on the phone, but voices sometimes sound different on the phone."

Not that much. "Do you think it could have been someone else? Did it sound like anyone else you know?"

She just shrugs.

"Okay, what did he say?"

"That if I didn't want to wind up back in Cartagena with my family, I'd keep my mouth shut. That I'd come home from school one day and my family wouldn't be there because he'd report them to immigration and they'd be deported. The last time he called he said he knew I was living in Queens and I should watch my back when I took the subway there or I'd wind up like Ripley."

"When was that?"

"Two nights ago."

Somebody knocks on the door, first one time, then a series of taps. I spring up and open it. A female uniformed officer hands me a sandwich wrapped in plastic. Julissa scowls as I place it in front of her. "No hamburger?"

"You didn't ask for a hamburger," I point out. Her fingers pull at the plastic and unfurl it, revealing two slices of multigrain bread. Julissa peels off the top slice. "Tuna," she says unenthusiastically and takes a bite. I remain standing.

How much more can I accomplish here? "Your parents, Julissa...where are they?"

She puts down her soggy sandwich and looks at me piercingly and says in a tear-choked voice, "I don't know!"

"You don't..."

"I told them to hide. I told them I heard that ICE was coming for them. I told them not to tell me where they were in case someone tried to get it out of me and that I'd stay with Leidy until it was safe."

"But you wouldn't be able to let them know it was safe."

"But they're not back there."

I hope not. "Is there anyone there who they might have been in contact with who would know where they are?"

Her attention diverts back to her sandwich. "I could really use a drink to wash this down," she says.

I know I'm going to need a drink, a strong one, to wash down the events of the last couple of days. I don't know what else I can do here. "One last thing and I'll get you that drink." I lean in conspiratorially. "Who told you nobody would believe you, Julissa?" I guess wildly. "Mrs. Wimbish?"

"Yes, her," Julissa nods. "And the shrink. She said I had to go to him or I wouldn't be allowed back in school. He said I was suffering from a personality disorder and nobody would believe me and I'd get far worse treatment if I got sent to a hospital, which he said he could arrange..."

"Those calls you got...did it sound like him on the phone, Julissa?"

She looks me straight in the eyes. "It sounded a lot like him."

I've done all I can here. I feel I'm leaving something out but having had little sleep and a near concussion will do that to you. Julissa at least confirmed who her perp was. Sick bastard. And it doesn't begin and end with him, but it ends for Julissa now at least. "Is Coke okay?" She nods and I slip out of the room again. "She wants a soda," I tell Gibson. "Make that a Big Gulp after what she's been through. She deserves it. And a lawyer."

40

I deserve a few hours of sleep after all of this, but by the time I get home to my apartment, it's almost noon and I promised to meet Freddie in Brooklyn at four. And I'm too wired to sleep anyway. I keep picturing Quick and Gibson showing up at GreenWood and fantasize the grilling Keaton and Mrs. Wimbish and Aubrey are overdue for, particularly Keaton, though I'd relish shaking down Aubrey myself. I asked f I could accompany them, to see her squirm when asked why she lied and sent me on a wild goose chase that could have gotten me killed. Quick said succinctly, "No. We'll handle her. We'll call you later." I think he suspects I would actually hurt her. I might have been tempted. So all I have to satisfy me are visions of justice served.

I know I should feel better about my role in this; I was the one who assigned the girls to do storyboards, which weren't even my own idea to begin with. I have to thank Heidi Obermeyer for that if she ever calls me for another modeling job. If not for that, Keaton would still be free to do God knows what to them without any fear of repercussion because he scared them shitless. He and Mrs. Wimbish, who looked the other way whenever it served her purpose and told anyone who complained, "It's not us, it's you" and sent them to the shrink. *And what a shrink at that.* I can't wait to hear how this all comes down. And even more, I can't wait to hear Freddie's account from inside the war zone. She is the only thing I miss about GreenWood, aka Clusterfuck Middle School.

I flip over the page of a sketch pad lying on the floor next to me and start doodling. I draw one, then two figures that evolve into female figures, which evolve into pubescent female figures. I give them hair flying in escape, eyes wide with fear, clothes strewn on the floor because they've been made to take them off. I can understand how drawing what they were hiding inside was so liberating for Violet and Julissa, yet more than they bargained for. I keep sketching, tear off one page, and start another one of a girl crossing her arms in front of her and then reaching her arms to the sky, exulting in freedom. I feel like I've run a 5 K and want to still keep going. I know what my next project will be.

I keep doing rough sketches on the theme, giving myself plenty to decide from later. I look at the sheaves of paper I've used and place them on my bed, face up, as if they were Tarot cards and I was about to do a reading. I have to leave if I want to get to Brooklyn and be on time to meet Freddie. I'm in a better frame of mind than I have been in weeks. All I need is resolution of all of this to be able to feel truly good about my role in it.

Without knowing what happened to Violet I'm not sure if anyone will have resolution. Even the flyers with her photo on them are beginning to go missing. I used to see several on my way to the West 4th Street subway station and now there are blank spaces and flyers advertising a live art installation and a seventy percent sale in a store around the block that has been going out of business forever; I guess now they really are. Violet was like a key that fell out of my hand and down through a street grating before I could insert it securely into a lock. She could be anywhere and I feel like everyone has all but given up on finding her. In my efforts to get Julissa to talk, I didn't think much about Violet myself. My eyes still scan faces passing in search for a girl with a streak of bright purple hair. Maybe she dyed it by now. If she hasn't died.

The subway platform is nearly deserted, but I still stand as far from the track as I can, something I'd done even before Ripley Herrera fell to her death practically in front of me, but even more since. My feet sense the rumbling of the A train approaching in the tunnel even before I see it and I count cars before positioning myself at a door. I don't want to be in the first car or the last. I slither behind a woman struggling with a wheelie suitcase and slide onto a seat near the door. Just in case. The doors slide shut and the train lurches into the tunnel. I pat the pouch on the outside of my tote to make sure I remembered my phone and take a deep breath. I don't want to miss my transfer and I check my watch. I should have left earlier. The address Freddie gave me isn't that close to GreenWood. Maybe it's closer to her home or where her brother receives care. She's been to my place, but I still have no idea where she lives. As soon as I get off the train, I'll call her to tell her I'm on my way. I pull the phone out of my pocket when I get off at Hoyt-Schermerhorn and stare at it as if just by doing so I'll pick up a signal. I'm too deep underground. And in too deep. Or I was, I remind myself. I was. The worst is over.

The G train is getting near rush hour full, even though it's before four. I look at the map on the car wall and count five stops, then squeeze into an available half a seat and squirm until the guy sitting next to me who looks like a Sumo wrestler gets up to get off at Fulton Street. I feel like a new New York transplant, finding my way around for the first time. When the train chortles into the Myrtle-Willoughby Avenues station, I leap up like I was sitting on a scorching andiron, drawing stares, eliciting a mumble of "crazy white chick." I hustle up the stairs to street level and pause to get oriented and pull my phone out of my pocket just as the voice mail alert chirps. No messages from Freddie. Two missed calls and a text in all capital letters from Quick. CALL ME.

I scurry away from pedestrian traffic and lean against a wrought-iron fence away from the stairwell and punch in his digits methodically. He picks up right away. "I tried calling..."

"I just saw. I was in the subway. What's going on?" I'm not sure if I'm ready for his answer.

"Keaton Jeffries played hooky today, it seems," he says. "No sign of him. But Gibson had a nice talk with that other girl, Aubrey. It seems she was currying favor with him, trying to be teacher's pet; she seems to have had a schoolgirl crush on him."

"Pardon me while I gag. What?"

"Apparently he rewarded her handsomely for baiting Julissa and landing her in detention. At least academically. She started getting good grades, in his class at least, but she hadn't always. Gibson asked to see some of her work. It wasn't exactly A material. She was being rewarded for something. Gibson asked if she'd ever had to stay in detention after school like Julissa and some of the other girls did and she said no. She almost seemed disappointed. She also left that little note on your stoop. She wanted to spook you."

"So I wouldn't get the school rapist busted? I wonder what was in the report cards for her for telling me where Julissa was in Jackson Heights? And how she found out because Julissa seems to hate her so she didn't tell her. Had I not gotten that call from Freddie that Julissa was busted for shoplifting, I would have walked right into..." I pause. "Bless her larcenous soul. Who killed the aunt...Leidy?"

"We don't know yet. Where are you?"

"On my way to meet Freddie. Did you...any of you... talk with her?"

"No, and we'd like to."

"Why?"

"She may have information pertinent to our investigation."

"Which she didn't have before?" I clear my throat. "Okay, okay, I'll tell her you just want her take on it."

"You could put it that way. Where are you meeting her?" I give him the address, just a few blocks from here. I hear a pause, long enough to make me think we've been disconnected. "Hello?"

"Okay, I have to go. I'll call back. Just be careful."

I'm putting my own spin on what they want, but I can't see Freddie being terribly willing to cooperate with the police, even if she knows my relationship with Quick. Even in the ninety plus degree heat, I feel a chill again. I start looking around me, looking for her, hoping for instant reassurance. It's entirely possible, even likely, I remind myself, that Freddie would dodge any reconnaissance with the police if she could, even for positive gains. Calling them on my behalf, to send them to my rescue, was a lot less threatening to her than a face to face. I've seen her face when she was face to face. I just want to see her face now.

I walk briskly by boarded-up-and-graffitied dollar stores and vacant houses with peeling siding. Almost in a blink, as if I stepped from one sound stage to another, the abandoned buildings morph into a block of well-kept salmon and vanilla colored brownstones with window grates and flower planters in lush bloom and wonder if Freddie lives in one of them. She said Bed-Stuy is the next Williamsburg and she's probably right. I was lucky enough to score a rent controlled sublet, in the West Village no less, inhabited by an art professor who hasn't gouged me, at least not yet. What will happen to Freddie if GreenWood closes and she's out of work? I cross the street and turn down the next left. The address she gave me is apparently down the end of the block and I keep walking past a couple of teenagers bouncing a basketball against a wall who eye me warily as I trudge toward the sandwich board sign on the sidewalk promising "a whole latte love for each other." The café is all blonde wood and ebony trim. There is limited seating inside and I can see at a glance that Freddie isn't here. I take out my phone and enter her number and immediately hear her voicemail message. "Freddie, where are you? Call me when you get this message. Sorry I was a little late. I'm waiting at the café. I'm getting a drink and...waiting." My mouth feels like it was scoured with a steel wool pad.

"Can I help you?"

I approach the counter and ask for an Iced Americano and check my phone for probably the hundredth time. As the barista hands me my change, I lock eyes with him. "Has anybody called...to say they'd be late? I was supposed to meet my friend here at four," I look at my watch. "And it's four twenty and I'm late but she'd have waited for me. I'm sure she would. She told me you know her here." I gulp. "Frederica Shaw."

The barista turns around and whispers something to the other barista making a cappuccino behind the counter. He nods and the first barista wheels around and says, "I'm new here, but Mustafa said he knows her." He hands me my drink, which I immediately guzzle and feel a satisfying cold burn as I swallow. I step back out of the way of other customers and look out through the storefront windows onto the street and watch people pass by. *No Freddie.*

Mustafa signals me over to the far end of the counter. "You're friends with Freddie Shaw?"

"I was supposed to meet her here at four and it's..." I check my watch again. "Four-thirty. She didn't call...to say she'd be late? I was on the G train so no calls were coming through." Though they certainly would have showed up when I got off the train at Myrtle-Willoughby. Quick's calls did.

Mustafa shakes his head with a rueful smile. "I wish I could say she did. Freddie's good people. She helps kids in the neighborhood a lot so what happened to her brother hopefully won't happen to them. You know about..."

I nod. "Maybe she's with him. Where do you think I could find them?" Mustafa raises his eyebrows slightly, as if questioning just how close our friendship is or if we're friends at all. I've got to go for broke. "We work together and one of our...colleagues," I almost gag on the word, "is wanted by the police and Freddie may be in danger. And maybe Rick, too, if she's with him."

"What's he wanted for?"

"Oh, rape...maybe murder...who knows what else."

Mustafa frowns and I wonder if, being a guy, he thinks I'm overdramatizing. I've been trying to convince myself that there could still be a logical explanation for Freddie to not be here, not an ominous one, but having been through what I have and knowing Keaton, it's a hard sell. Why wasn't he at the school today? I thought he was being watched. And why couldn't the police track down Freddie if she was there. *If she was there.* Freddie seems infinitely more capable of defending herself than his usual fourteen-year-old prey, but still.

"Maybe you should check if she's home?" I must look as blank as the sandwich board sign that the other barista just erased because Mustafa hastily jots down what looks to be an address on the back of a cookie envelope and slides it over to me. "About three blocks north of here. It's an off-white three family walk-up. Very off-white because it's dirty. Damn slumlord does shit. She's my neighbor, but I don't see her coming and going that much. Different schedules. I didn't see her the last two days, but that doesn't mean nothing. If she's not there, try this," Mustafa pulls the envelope back and writes down another address. "That's the assisted living home where Rick is. If she's not at the first, she's probably at the second. If she's not there, I don't know what to tell you." His voice trails off. "I hope she's there."

"So do I," I slip a dollar bill in the tip jar and swig the rest of my drink and drop the cup in the trash receptacle right outside the door. I don't believe Freddie would stand me up. Not unless she had a damn good reason and I'm afraid of what that reason might be.

41

Nobody is answering the door at la casa Shaw. I know I'm knocking on the right door because Freddie's name is one of the few still adhered securely on the mailbox next to the doorbell and a new issue of Vogue and plain manila envelope addressed to her are on the chipped linoleum floor. There was no answer when I rang her doorbell so I rang random bells until I got buzzed in. I don't hear any activity behind the painted white door or anywhere else on the floor. I knock again. "Freddie?" Nothing.

I try turning the knob but the door is locked, which is a relief because I don't know how I'd feel about invading Freddie's personal space, even out of worry and fear. I'll call Quick when I leave the building, before I go to the assisted living residence and let him know she isn't answering the door. I hear creaking on the stairs behind me, like somebody is trudging home after a long day. "Freddie?"

The creaking stops. My heart does a sort of flutter like it does after too much caffeine, which of course I had. I raise my fist to knock again and stop in midair. Who am I kidding? She's not there. I hurriedly punch in her number on my phone. Voicemail again. I tap END CALL and slide my phone in my pocket and turn around to leave the way I came when I hear creaking again. I pivot and walk down to the other end of the hall on tiptoe, trying not to make any noise. I peer out the window. Fire escape. Great. All I have to do is open the window and do it quietly. I give it a quick thrust hoping it'll glide right up, but the wood is swollen from the heat and stuck in its tracks and isn't budging. Whoever is on the stairwell is more than taking their sweet time. If it were a person who lived here, they'd have been in their apartment by now, even with two broken legs. My instincts are screaming at me to run, but my legs seem not to have gotten the message.

The door to my right has no number on it and as I touch the knob, it springs open, leading to a dark stairwell. I start down slowly, careful not to make any noise, taking one step at a time, again on tiptoe. Nobody can approach without my knowing they're coming and then I could speed up. I descend the second flight of steps more quickly, not turning back. I can see light reflections on the ground level stairs. Just one more flight.

I suddenly trip on something underfoot and miss two stairs and balance myself against the wall to keep from falling further and bite my lip to keep from crying out. I bend down to inspect what was there, a narrow spindly thing that looks like it came off a lizard. I frown. It's a stiletto heel from a shoe. The rest of the shoe and its twin are on the landing down below. Those are Freddie's prized Louboutins, her favorites. She would never shed those without a fight. There had to be one hell of a fight. I scramble down and pick them up and cram them in my bag, broken heel and all. I turn the knob to the door leading outside and propel myself forward and find myself face to face with Dr. Zimmerman as I catch a huge whiff of his cologne.

"If you're looking for Miss Shaw, she's not home," he says.

"So I noticed. Where is she and what did you do to her?"

His eyes narrow. "I have no interest in doing anything to Miss Shaw. She hasn't done anything to merit bad treatment."

And I have? Great.

"Are you feeling all right, Miss Price? You seem flushed."

"It's hard to believe why I would be—it's only something like ninety-five degrees." I gulp, weighing my options. If I stay here, I'm a dead duck. If I try to run, I'm probably still a dead duck. If I make a lot of noise and draw attention, maybe somebody will look away from their pick up basketball game or dime bag deal or dinner cooking on the stove and report it, giving me a fighting chance. I underestimated how physically imposing Zimmerman could be. I feel like I'm railing up against a brick wall, albeit a roughly 5'7" one. How'd he get here without my seeing him like I did in Jackson Heights, unless he was here ahead of me, waiting? But how would he know I was supposed to meet Freddie unless she told him. She wouldn't tell him. Not even under duress. I can't believe she would. I'm afraid to ask.

I decide to bolt quickly, but he is even quicker, wrestling me to the dirty floor and pinning my arm behind me. I'm reminded of when I was accosted when I was leaving his office the day of the school shooting. I feel a sharp jab. *Him and his damn needles.* He got me this time. I feel like my head is a watermelon, too large and heavy to lift, and my mouth tastes metallic. I feel myself lifted and I am suddenly floating, suspended, a marionette without strings, flailing my limbs in slow motion. I'm on one hell of a trip. My head tilts back into a cloud of feathers and a sunbeam shines on my face. Or rather it's a pupil gauge directed into my eyes. The cloud is a hospital-issue pillow and the screech of a siren makes me realize I'm in an ambulance. Good, I think, I was saved. I don't remember being saved but I obviously was if I'm in an ambulance and being tended to.

I open my eyes and recognize the receptionist from Zimmerman's office hovering over me. "She's waking up, Egon."

"Give her more Brevital," he barks from behind me and I realize with a start that he is driving the ambulance. So much for being saved. I smell alcohol as the receptionist swabs my arm with a prep pad and try jerking away, but nothing happens. I open my mouth to ask how she's even qualified to administer drugs, but nothing comes out. What are they giving me? It strikes me as hugely ironic that they're such sticklers for sterile conditions when they seem bent on doing something nasty to me. They might as well spit on it. I close my eyes and feel like I'm drifting on a cloud again, albeit a cumulonimbus, with lights flashing and siren wailing.

42

When I open my eyes, I can't see anything. I'm blind, I think in a panic. He gave me something to blind me. Then I realize that I see specks of light in the far corner of wherever I am, light cheating its way past some sort of fabric blocking what are probably windows. I focus on the light, trying to make out shapes and then objects. I try to reach out but I can't move my arms. They feel like they're pinned in front of me. I shouldn't be surprised. I'm surprised I wasn't blindfolded, but then what is here for me to see? I try to take a step forward but my legs are tied together too. Nope, not surprised. I clear my throat. I realize I'm not gagged, but that only tells me there's no one around to hear me who could actually help me. I realize I can't hear anything outside either that would help me guess where I am, not a single car go by, a bird tweeting, anything.

"Who's there?" a soft voice asks.

"Who are you?"

"Delilah?" I recognize that voice; it's Freddie. I can't see her, but she can't be too far from me. As I get used to the minimal light, I can see that there are partitions set up, much like the privacy screens in hospitals, but the atmosphere as in the ambulance is only marginally clinical. I feel like I wandered into a theater of the absurd production of *One Flew Over The Cuckoo's Nest*, only it's the doctor who's the cuckoo one. I have no idea why we're here or what he wants with us, but it can't be good. I can't walk or even stand, but I can try to at least roll, leaning hard on my left side and landing on my stomach. I take as deep a breath as I can and try to flip again. No go. I can make out a cot set up next to me and I'm not sure why I'm not on it. Maybe I fell off of it or maybe he didn't have the slightest intention of making me comfortable.

"Delilah, is that you?" Freddie's voice sounds stronger now. "Are you okay?"

"Are you?"

"I asked first."

I have to hand it to her; she's made me smile for the first time since I put down my charcoal pencil in my apartment earlier today. Or was it yesterday? I realize I'm not sure how much time has passed. Zimmerman could have been pumping drugs into us indefinitely. "I'm okay, I think," I say, wanting to reassure myself that that's true.

"I'm sorry I couldn't meet you. I got...tied up."

"What is this fucking thing?" I wriggle and feel like the vise has tightened around me. I'm not sure if I should try to free my legs or arms first or if I can do either. When I scrunch my shoulders, I feel a little give; that makes me feel better, like maybe if I keep working at it, I'll get somewhere. But first I need to be sure there is somewhere to get and that I have enough time to get there without being discovered. And I have to take Freddie with me.

"I believe it's what they call a straitjacket if you're talking about the same thing that I've got on. What does he want from us?" Freddie asks.

That's what I'd like to know. Not once has Zimmerman given any hint where he fits in, what the stakes are for him, but for him to badger and blackmail a fourteen-year-old patient and for me to see him in the proximity of a murder scene, they have to be pretty high. Julissa outed Keaton as the person she depicted in her drawing, but where does Zimmerman fit into the picture? Even with the picture blurry to me right now, he's right in there.

"He didn't say anything to me, but I was out of it."

"So was I. I was on my way to school. Just headed out the door and a pillowcase was thrown over my head and I tried doing a judo move on him and..."

"You lost your Louboutins. It's okay. I found them. I have them." At least I had them. I can only assume that Zimmerman took custody of my bag and everything in it. I don't have the heart to tell her one was broken. That's the least of what could get broken here and I know it. I close my eyes and imagine Quick calling me or trying to; all calls would go directly to voice mail, as mine to Freddie did. I try to conjure scenarios that would lead him here, wherever here is, and I wonder if he weren't obsessed with the ABC rapist if he would have been more on top of this.

What if the guy the cops have all been looking for has been right under their noses all along? I hear soft footsteps approaching somewhere behind me. "Here he comes," Freddie says softly. "Keep him busy. I'm going to try something."

"What?"

"Shhhhh," Freddie's shushes turn into a hiss that accompanies a door squeaking open. The footsteps are not soft any more. What if ABC is Zimmerman? He has very definitely been involved in the students' lives in a very mentally unhealthy way, but nobody has implicated him in anything sexual with them or with adults. *At least not yet.* Maybe they were drugged and didn't know. I gasp as the inside door rattles open. I get an immediate whiff of cloying cologne and cough in response. My throat feels like I gargled with it. Zimmerman seems oblivious to my discomfort or maybe he's enthralling in it.

"How are we feeling?' he asks, his voice dripping with condescension. He aims a pupil gauge at one eye, then the other. I blink like I've seen a flash go off. I have no desire to make this any easier for him than it already has been. He already got me here. Now I want answers.

"I would be feeling a lot better if I were home, like I should have been by now. Whatever time now is."

"I'm sure you would," he says. "It's a beautiful day out there. Want to take a look?" He yanks down the crepey black fabric that covered the window closest to me and the light sears my eyes. All I can see is light, bright unrelenting light, no shapes or shadows of anything that might give me any idea of where we are. But I can see the room he's got us in more clearly now, set up like an impromptu hospital ward. "And I'm sure Miss Shaw would rather be with her brother and could have been, had you minded your own business. She only has you to blame for her being here."

"Where exactly are we?" I ask. "And why?"

Zimmerman frowns. "I suppose you have a right to know why I've brought you here. Don't worry about where here is too much. You may not stay here and at any rate you won't be able to get away no matter where I bring you."

He crouches down. "You persisted in encouraging your students to implicate that a fellow teacher, a respected teacher, was guilty of aberrant behavior. These students, who all suffer from borderline personality disorders and worse..."

"Making them easy to take advantage of," I point out. "Along with their immigration status and sexual precociousness." Even if my mouth weren't dry and my throat parched and sore. I'd find his description of Keaton as respected hard to swallow. "All I did was assign them storyboards. I didn't know what their stories were. They told me. Their artwork did anyway. The truth was there." I pause to catch my breath. "What's it to you?"

"Keaton is my son," Zimmerman says, as if I should have known all along. And maybe I should have hazarded a guess. Keaton went running to his daddy after he got shot. I remember Freddie telling me that. We just didn't know who his daddy was or the means he had at his disposal to cover for him. A lot of clichés crowd into my mind. Chip off the old block. The apple doesn't fall far from the tree. Like father, like son? How alike are they and which one is worse? I'm afraid I'm about to find out.

Keep talking, I think, *keep talking*. I have the right to find out the whole story before I go down and maybe I'm being looked for by now. I have to buy extra time. *Keep talking*.

"Where's his mother. If you don't mind my asking?"

"Dead. She died many years ago." I frown. I remember Keaton saying something about going to visit his mother in the hospital weeks ago. One of his alibis. Somebody is lying. Probably both of them.

"So where is he?"

"I thought you were concerned about where you are," Zimmerman says.

"That too," I agree, licking my lips with whatever moisture I can summon. I need a drink of water badly, but I'm afraid of what he could put in it and even if I did have a drink, how would I then be able to pee? Zimmerman would probably be only too happy to stand by and watch until my bladder exploded. I wonder if Keaton is here, wherever here is, channel surfing or kicking back with a beer, wearing his red B—as in bastard—baseball cap, content in the knowledge that his daddy has everything under control. Zimmerman scrutinizes me like he's still trying to decide how to get rid of me. Getting me here was apparently easy. I can only guess more drugs are in my future.

"I smelled you in my friend Sachi's apartment. And in the subway station where that girl Ripley was pushed in

front of a train. I smelled you when I got mugged in the
vestibule after I first came to see you after the shooting
at GreenWood. I keep smelling a rat and it's you. If you
thought you could get away with any of this, at least you
could have ditched the cologne."

"Who's Sachi?" he asks,

I realize that Keaton must have borrowed his father's
toiletries for some of his own after-curricular activities. I
guess he didn't tell daddy everything.

"Ask Keaton who Sachi is. If he remembers. Who
knows how many he did this to?" No matter what I think
of Sachi now and that their first sex was apparently con-
sensual, rape is still rape. "I guess grown-up girls were too
much for him after her and Deidre Marx so he went back to
his seventh graders. Easier game. Why are you covering for
him anyway? Don't you think this all indicates he's a wee
bit crazy? Shouldn't you be getting help for him instead?"

"I did. She made him worse. I'm the only one who can
manage him."

And a fine job you've done. I try not to show my exasperation. Every word I say to him is going to come back to
get me but I have to get some answers while I can "How
did he get a job teaching in a school with teenage girls?"

"He has excellent academic credentials. Fordham.
Harvard."

"And no record?"

"His youthful transgressions were expunged." I wonder by whom and what he means by transgressions. Anything short of murder? "He was eminently qualified. How
he ended up in GreenWood specifically is I did Mrs. Wimbish a big favor. I pulled some strings for her to get the kind
of care she needed for her daughter and she pulled some
strings for me. Her daughter was born with spina bifida
and a whole host of other congenital abnormalities, needs

round-the-clock care, and she wanted her at home. She has
a live-in nurse and the kind of care she'd likely never get in
an institution, which is where she'll wind up if GreenWood
is closed. A place like where Miss Shaw's brother is, where
patients can lie for days in their own urine if they're not
lucky enough to have a sister like Miss Shaw."

I hear Freddie croak, "Fuck you!"

He ignores her. "Wimbish kept an eye on him and notified me any time there was a problem with Keaton."

"There were several I'm aware of. How many others?"

"Nothing we couldn't handle."

I roll my eyes. "You're a psychiatrist...supposedly. You
couldn't see how much damage that was doing to these girls...
and you were treating them? No conflict of interest there."

"You've never seen Chloe Wimbish."

"Did you happen to see Ripley Herrera after the 6 train
ran over her?"

His expression is as good as a guilty plea. His face pales,
more sweat beads on his forehead, he licks his lips. "I saw
Keaton on the platform and I was afraid he was going to do
something rash and ruin his future. She was pregnant and
she was going to ruin him. He threatened he would kill her..."

"So you did instead." I swallow hard. His eyes bore into
me like a laser. "What was he thinking, knocking up a fourteen-year-old girl?"

"She seduced him."

"I doubt that. Did she tell him she was pregnant?"

"Yes, him and that buttinsky teacher of hers, the one
you replaced, Deidre Marx. She came to my office like you
did, not knowing Keaton is my son, just as you didn't, but
thinking that since I was the girls' mental health provider, I
could help since no one at the school would."

"And you certainly did, didn't you?" I feel my face flush.
I was lucky to have gotten away that first time. Otherwise

nobody might have ever known. All the storyboards would have been destroyed. "Okay, so who else did Keaton knock up? Oh, wait, he probably learned his lesson from this, didn't he, and only insisted on blow jobs."

"That would be prudent. No DNA."

"That remains to be seen." I think of the thong I found in the school closet, the thong that DNA results haven't come back on yet, last I knew, the thong hopefully loaded with semen or hairs or something, the thong that might have been Julissa's or belonged to somebody else who made the mistake of crossing his path, crossing him. How many made that mistake?

"Any other questions, Miss Price?"

"What happened to Violet Velez?"

"Oh, yes, the purple haired one, the cutter, the one whose boyfriend opened fire." His expression makes me feel sick to my stomach, or maybe it's the drugs he's been pumping into me, or a combination of the two. "Didn't I see on the news that the police found her belongings near the river, that she was presumed drowned?" He definitely more than presumes. *Poor Violet.* I try to lick my lips again but my mouth is completely dry. "Water," I croak. "Could I have a drink of water?"

"Yes, I think I can get that for you," he says, turning to the door behind him, scrutinizing me, maybe evaluating whether water will accelerate or retard whatever he plans to do with me next. He gets up slowly from his crouching position and stands still for a moment, hovering over me, then strides to the door and leaves it slightly ajar behind him. I try to pull myself into a sitting position.

"Is he gone?" Freddie asks behind the partition. Even though she spoke barely above a whisper, she sounds stronger now. Her voice seems closer.

"Not far," I answer hoarsely. "Just to get me some water...if I can swallow it."

"Well, you might not want to swallow all of it."

"What?"

"Ssssh," Freddie shushes me. "When I say, 'Can I please have a drink of water too?', take a drink but don't swallow it. Spit it in his face."

"And get killed?"

"I freed myself," she says. "Leave everything to me"

43

"What? You did? How?"

"I'll tell you later. I think I hear him coming back."

I take a deep breath and steel myself for this next showdown, imagining how everything could go horribly wrong. Zimmerman enters the room bearing a metal tray with a glass of water resting on top, but that's not all; I see a pill container, a syringe and two ampoules filled with pink tinged fluid. He places the tray on the floor and crouches close to me. "You're not going to remember anything about our conversation," Zimmerman says matter-of-factly, almost pleasantly. He pops open the unmarked pill vial and shakes two out into his palm. "I'm putting these in your mouth and you'll swallow them. If you don't swallow them, we'll have to get this into you the other way."

"My mouth is so dry," I whisper. "I don't think I can swallow anything unless I have a drink first." I cough. "And it won't work unless it dissolves... right?"

He ogles the syringe. "Maybe we should just do it this way."

"Can I please have a fucking drink of water?"

Zimmerman glowers at me, no doubt thinking what difference could it possibly make if I'm hydrated before he knocks me out or not. He finally slides his hand under my head and lifts it so I won't gag. He holds the glass up to my lips and I stick out my tongue at it first, lapping it slowly like a parched dog, then take a mouthful and let it sit there in my cheeks, afraid to swallow it, afraid that the water may be doctored too.

I hear Freddie clear her throat. "Can I please have a drink of water too?"

I spew the water out of my mouth, not exactly in a perfect stream, but hitting my target. "Goddamn!" he bellows. Water glistens in the creases of Zimmerman's eyes and drips off his stubby lashes. He raises his arm to wipe himself dry and reaches for the syringe on the tray and jams the needle into the ampoule, retracting the plunger and filling the syringe, giving it a little squirt in the air. He turns back to me and grabs my arm, aiming the needle like a dart, hovering over the crook in my arm, not seeing Freddie gaining on him in three swift silent strides. "Hurry!" I mouth to her. I feel the needle just touch the skin over my bicep, like a teasing wasp, not sure whether I'm worth stinging or not. I brace myself for a jab. Before he can drive it home, Freddie wraps her arm around his neck and gives his arm a quick chop. The syringe thuds to the floor, inches away from my face. Zimmerman staggers back, losing his balance for just the second that Freddie needs to give him another chop, this time to his jaw, and Freddie and Zimmerman literally butt heads reaching for it. Zimmerman's arm flails in front of me, right in my face, one finger under my nose. I jut my head back and bite down hard. Zimmerman screams. Freddie grabs the syringe and jams it into his arm through his shirt and pushes in the plunger. Zimmerman rolls on his back and exhales with a hiss, an overblown balloon popped. His eyes flutter closed.

"Well, that worked," Freddie says with a satisfied smile, though I can see her shaking. "I don't know how long we've got though. We've got to get out of here."

"Wherever here is,"

Freddie stoops down and unbuckles and unfastens me. "The very latest in S & M wear," she says, casting the straitjacket to one side and helping me up. "Are you okay?"

I nod uncertainly, stretching my arms in front of me and flexing my knees. "He doesn't look so good. Is...is he breathing?"

Freddie frowns. "Shit, I don't know. What the fuck was he going to shoot us up with?"

"Let's get out of here." I pull the door wide open and shakily lead the way down the hall, stepping over plaster chips and sawdust. A bathroom is to my left and another room with no furniture to my right, all with peeling paint and wallpaper. I turn around to see how Freddie is doing maneuvering barefoot over the debris. As I start down a narrow staircase to my right, a chunk of plaster drops out of a large crack in the wall and crumbles into dust on the floor. "Hurry before this whole place collapses." I feel like I'm swaying. I grab the banister to steady myself and feel it wobble. "Hurry." Freddie passes me and holds my other arm as we descend the last of the stairs. Drop cloths cover the floor and a couple of ladders stand up against peeling walls. Freddie turns the crystal doorknob facing us and the door heaves open and hangs on one hinge.

The pink stucco exterior, contrasted with the horror inside, looks like something out of Architectural Digest, fitting in well with what I can see of a couple of other houses in the distance, all polished and buffed and manicured, awe-inspiring during a drive-by, and innocuous enough to not warrant any sort of investigation. Who would suspect anyone living here of harboring hostages? I gesture for Freddie to follow me as I walk around to the side of the house, next to a winding driveway, looking for the way out to the street.

"Hey, Delilah, what's that?" Freddie gestures toward something multicolored in the bushes that doesn't quite blend in with the wilting roses and begonias planted there. I walk over to it gingerly and then quicken my pace.

"It's my bag. Holy shit!" I free it from its prickly rose bush bed with a tug and pull up the flap and grope around inside for my phone, but the pocket I kept it in is empty and it's not jostling around when I shake it. I get down on my knees and grope around with my hand and find the shoe with no heel and then the other. "Look, Freddie! Your shoes!"

"Even I can't wear those here," she says, kicking aside gravel with her perfectly pedicured feet. Even in escape mode, she looks like a runway model; I'll bet she really could wear them even here, if not for the missing heel. I toss them back in my bag and then feel around some more, but all I feel are rose thorns. I don't know what else is missing. I sling the bag over my arm and start down the driveway again, looking for a path to the street. "Where are we?"

I hear the screech of brakes somewhere behind me and guess that the street has to be in the direction that sound came from and then see a midnight blue Jaguar lurch into view, careening from the driveway onto the lawn toward us, Keaton Jeffries behind the wheel. *So much for pristine gardening.*

"We're in deep shit is where we are," Freddie says. "Run!"

I dart in the direction I was walking and glance back only briefly to make sure Freddie is right behind me. I hear a car door slam and push myself to run harder but I can't; my muscles feel like somebody is playing tug of war with them. Pain shoots through my ribcage and I wonder if Zimmerman did something to me while I was unconscious or if I'm having a heart attack. I haven't eaten or drank anything, save for that sip of water I spit back in Zimmerman's face, since I had that Café Americano yesterday. If it was even yesterday. I hear a yelp behind me. "Freddie?" I cry out. "Freddie?"

I turn around. Freddie scrambles up from being down on all fours and then she cries out in pain. "Keep going!" she screams. I hear rustling behind me and the thud of footsteps as I cross back onto a gravel part of the driveway. There are two of us versus one of him, I remind myself. He can't take us both down. This is something I'm sure he wasn't counting on. Otherwise he would have had a weapon with him. His father has been so efficient at eliminating any possible threats to him that he never imagined he'd be in any danger, just doing mop up work. *Up to now.* My knees buckle and I fall forward, landing on the dirt and gravel with a thud. Keaton lands on top of me and pins my arms behind me. He flips me over. "I can take you right here, right now." He reaches between my legs and pulls my pants to one side and I feel a finger thrust inside me. My skin feels like something is crawling all over me and it doesn't help that I'm lying splay legged on the ground and something probably is crawling all over me, in addition to Keaton. I take as deep a breath as I can and bring up my knee and shove it into him, right below the Gucci belt. The double G buckle gores my skin. I bite my lower lip to brace myself for more pain as I knee him again. He withdraws his hand and curls up, writhing. I notice he had unzipped himself. Yep, I note with satisfaction, that's got to hurt.

I scramble to my feet and back step as fast as I can manage and pull Freddie up. "I think I twisted something," she whimpers. "I can't put weight on my right leg."

"Well, heels are definitely out for you then," I whisper. She manages a weak smile and then cowers. I spin around and see Keaton standing inches away from us. He whips his belt out of its loops and begins to spin it like a lariat, slowly at first, then faster, and then lashes it at us, first me, then Freddie, the buckle smashing right below her left cheekbone, then me again. I duck but he comes at me again, lashing across my shoulders. "I'm going to have fun with the both of you," he snarls. "Who wants to be first?"

"I would think you'd think we're too old for you. Can't get it up with women older than, say, fifteen is what I heard," I say.

"Says who?"

"Sachi Kitani," I watch for a reaction. Does he even remember who Sachi was?

"Oh, her," he smiles tightly. "The Asian one who liked it rough. Don't worry. I got it up."

"So you acknowledge you raped her."

"I had sex with her. She didn't exactly resist. She invited me up. And it wasn't the first time." He smirks. "You still owe me from our last date, Frederica. And you..." he gestures to me. "I'm not done with you. Hurts, doesn't it?" He whips the belt across my back this time. I gasp and fall on my stomach, peering up through blades of grass to see him on his hands and knees lowering himself on top of Freddie. Raising myself even an inch sends stinging pain down each nerve. I start to wriggle on my stomach in the direction of my bag like I'm doing boot camp maneuvers. "Spread your legs, damn it," he growls behind me. I take it Freddie isn't being cooperative. *Good for her.* She yelps in pain. My hand shakes as I retrieve her shoe, one of her favorite reptile Louboutins, from my bag. I tuck it under my arm, and slither back, edging closer. Keaton looks up. "Anxious? Don't worry, you'll get your turn."

I hoist myself up on my elbows, then in a kneeling position, and aim the heel at his eye. He raises his hand defensively, but I plunge it as far as I can relentlessly, grimacing at the sound coming from his face, a macabre sound, like the exaggerated squishing of a bug on a cartoon, followed by a piercing scream. Blood rolls down his face and he reaches both hands up to try to assess what is going on. I kick him off Freddie and she reaches for his belt and ties his hands together. "Good job."

"What's that?" I frown, trying to make out a distant hum. I look up at the sky behind me and shield my eyes from the sun.

"Traffic helicopter," Freddie says, starting to wave her arms.

"There's no traffic," I point out. At least I haven't heard any traffic in all the time we've been outside. "Police helicopter!" I join in waving my arms. Every muscle on my body smarts and my skin stings. My head throbs. I take a deep breath, marveling that the hot humid air smells so good. Sirens pierce the silence of the neighborhood. Two NYPD blue and whites pull in the driveway, followed by two state police cars, followed by two unmarked cars, a veritable Noah's Ark of law enforcement. I see Quick walking across the lawn toward me and I'm not sure if I should love him or hate him.

"Are you okay?" he asks me.

"I've been better, I've been worse," I shrug. "Zimmerman's upstairs, he's..." I shrug and suddenly feel like I just disembarked from the Wonder Wheel at Coney Island. Quick summons EMTs over and I hesitate. "That's how he got me here."

"This is a legit bus, I promise. We'll talk later." He sizes up Freddie.

"You need a ride too."

"I'll ride with her," she says. "What are you going to do about him?" She gestures toward Keaton, lying on the grass, groaning. Gibson struts past us and replaces the belt tether with handcuffs. Two bulky EMTs hoist him on a stretcher and take him to another ambulance.

"Get in," Quick says as he nods for the paramedics to attend to me, not a second too soon. I feel like I'm going to be sick.

"Is my bag here?"

"I got it."

"Did I wreck your shoe?"

"The other one was broken anyway. And it was a worthwhile sacrifice," Freddie reassures me. "He's such a *heel.*"

44

"We have to stop meeting like this," I say when Quick sidles into my hospital room after visiting hours have ended.

"I brought you something," he says, reaching into his pocket and pulling out a new phone, much like mine was, only bigger. He hands it to me and I turn it on.

"Nice. Thanks."

He clears his throat and looks down at the floor, a petulant little boy, then looks straight at me with a laser stare. "I'm sorry this happened to you. The last address you gave me was the café and they were closed so we had to track down someone who worked there to see if anyone had seen you or knew where you were headed. When we got to Freddie's building, there were signs of a struggle, but there were other things going on by then and the scene became contaminated."

"Apology accepted." I swallow hard. "It's not like I have built in GPS. So how did you find out...?"

"We paid a visit to Dr. Zimmerman's office in the morning. He couldn't see us, the receptionist said, he was..."

"Booked solid!" I finish. "She was in on it, she was there when he took me..."

He nods. "Let me finish," he says. "So we ask for the appointment log and she says, not without a warrant. Which ate some more time, but we got one and tried to reach each person scheduled to see the good doctor, except for one slight problem. All of the numbers are either not in service or reassigned. All of the people whose names were written in the appointment log are dead."

"Which doesn't mean they aren't...weren't...crazy." I snipe. "You'd have to be to even go to him. Did he have any real patients? I mean, aside from the students..." I frown. "How did he pull it off? How was he making any money?"

"He was raking in the bucks for a while. There were lots of false claims for treatment that was probably not even needed, therapy for these girls lasted minutes and usually resulted in a prescription for Adderall or Valium or something similar and was billed for hours of intensive therapy. He saw Violet, the girl who cut herself, for at most five minutes every week and billed for an hour. He benefited from an in-home therapy scheme that provided minimal assistance to patients whose families thought it was a godsend to keep them home with them and some even got perks and weren't willing to blow the whistle on him. Some were threatened if they thought about it."

"Mrs. Wimbish," I utter, nodding. "She bent over backwards to keep his smarmy son on staff."

"She's not going to be too pleased about being reassigned, if she's reassigned at all. She's under investigation as well and if she in any way profited, she'll be playing principal in Bedford Hills."

"Where did he bring us, exactly?" I ask. "That house..."

"It was part of his scheme, a 'country psychiatric retreat' in Riverdale, only there was a lien put on it and he abandoned it. But not entirely. It's highly probable Zimmerman brought Deidre Marx there and then Keaton disposed of her in Inwood Hill Park. Very convenient."

"How many others did he...did they bring there?"

"We don't know yet," he says. "But we do know that neither of them was the ABC rapist."

"Is Zimmerman..."

"He went into cardiac arrest."

"Before he could be arrested."

"Exactly."

"Did he...rape anybody himself?"

Quick starts to shake his head, but stops. "His DNA wasn't an exact match to any we recovered from any of the victims involved, but there were familial similarities. He was definitely Keaton Jeffries' father. Keaton's DNA was all over the place. There were traces of him on Ripley Herrera, Julissa, Violet..."

"You found Violet?"

"No. Her family provided some of her underwear they found in her room. Julissa brought some in too. That thong wasn't hers. It belonged to Deidre Marx, the substitute teacher that we found in Inwood. She was also loaded with fentanyl."

"It was a joint effort," I mumble. "Like we would have been. Where does the receptionist come in? Why was she along for the ride?"

"She was in too deep to get out. She was terrified of Zimmerman and what he would do if she went to the authorities. She isn't in the country legally either and it's not certain that ICE will cut her a U visa deal since she was much more involved in Zimmerman's scheme. Julissa was just a scared shitless kid. Her family rematerialized, by the way."

"What a miracle," I say. "She knew where they were all the time, I'm sure."

"After what happened to her aunt, we can't blame her for zipping up. Zimmerman's DNA was at that apartment. Not on Leidy, but elsewhere. Julissa was the intended target. She was causing too much trouble. Leidy would have been collateral damage, no matter what."

"What happens to Keaton now?"

"He won't be seeing daylight any time soon, if ever." He pauses. "Through his good eye anyway."

I nod. "The ABC rapist..."

"He hasn't struck since early June. But no, we haven't identified or apprehended him yet. I was hoping it would turn out to be Jeffries too."

"So more round-the-clock task force work?"

"Not like before. Some officers from other precincts are joining the task force. Some are being reassigned. We'll get him."

I nod. "I'm sure you will."

"I'm sorry," he says again. "One other thing. You asked if Zimmerman raped anybody and I said no, which is to say he didn't rape any of the victims involved in this case. But before we went to his office, a woman came to the station, a psychiatrist, and asked to speak with me. She said that an incident happened years ago, when she was a fellow at a Boston teaching hospital—that Zimmerman raped her. The statute of limitations in Massachusetts is fifteen years and she never filed a complaint, but she thought we might need to know that."

45

After fiddling with my new smartphone for a couple of days, I think I've reloaded all of the apps I remember having had on my old phone and most of the contacts. I only minimally programmed it when Quick gave it to me. Looking at the glare from the screen for too long makes me feel bleary eyed, but I can tell I'm improving; when I was still in the hospital, I couldn't look at it for more than a couple of minutes without feeling woozy and I've been at it now for the good part of a half hour and just started having to turn away and I don't feel nauseous anymore. Progress.

Almost as if on cue, to test me further, it rings and I scowl at the default ring tone that sounds like a toddler banging on a xylophone. I obviously have more work ahead of me. Whoever is calling hasn't been added to my contact list. "Hi, Miss P? It's Julissa Dias!"

"Hi, Julissa, how are you? What's happening with you?"

"Plenty. I don't have to go back to Colombia and my family can stay too. They came out of hiding after they found out we weren't going to be deported." I don't ask her if she knew all along where they were. I'm happy for her. "And I think I might want to go to a school where I can do more art. I liked it."

I think I feel my heart flutter. "That's great, Julissa. But I have to tell you, if you want to apply to an arts high school or specialized program, you're going to have to not play hooky so much next year." And not shoplift. That goes without saying. "If you put a portfolio together, I'll look at it and make a recommendation based on that. When you're ready."

"Thanks!" She doesn't say a word about what she experienced. I think of what her reaction would be if she knew the extent of the battle Freddie and I were in for our lives, the epitome of GURL POWER. I hang up with a sigh of smug satisfaction. It's good to know I wasn't a total failure in the classroom.

But I never want to do that again.

My phone screen goes dark and I tap the home button, enter my code and start scrolling through my apps again and I stop short. I see one I know I never bought or downloaded, something called Sculptor Pro. I scroll down the menu and see anatomical figures whose poses can change with a click, a dimension scale, pretty much everything I need, everything but the studio space to actually translate what I create into three-dimensional form.

I mouth the words 'thank you' silently.

The phone plays the banging xylophone again. "Girlfriend," Freddie says. "Are you up for coffee? I can meet you in your 'hood in about an hour. So you don't have to come out here."

"I'd love it," I say and spend the next half hour updating my ringtones. The café Freddie suggested is two doors down from the bar we first went to, where we were challenged to darts by Keaton and ran off on him, stiffing him with the tab for the beer. At least there are no steep steps here. Neither of us is up to that.

"How do you walk in those things?" I tease Freddie as she glides over to the café table carrying a tray with two frozen lattes. "Ballet slippers?"

She laughs merrily. "No stilettos until my ankle completely heals, doctor's orders. At least a couple more weeks. These are not half bad now that I can put weight on it again, but I miss my Jimmy Choos. Not to mention my Louboutins. How are you doing?"

I shrug. "Okay, mostly."

"And Detective Quick, how are things with you and him?"

"Getting back to the way they were, I think," I say, though I'm not sure if that's entirely positive news. Where we were and where we are now is anybody's guess, but I still want to give it more time to find out. "And you, aside from that?" I lean in. "When we were on that lawn, did he...."

She shakes her head with a wicked grin. "Nope. He couldn't get it up."

"The power of suggestion," I sigh.

"So what are you going to do next?" Freddie asks. "I mean, when you feel better?"

"I feel okay. Some post-concussion symptoms, but they're going away. I am not teaching again." I survey the baristas at the counter, steaming milk for cappuccinos. "I should really waitress."

"I've heard that before." Freddie says. "Not even summer school?"

"No, definitely not."

"Adult Ed then,"

"Absolutely not, no, never."

"Aside from what happened, you really were very good at it," she points out. Julissa confirmed that during her earlier phone call, but I don't want to hear any more about it.

"I've got to find studio space," I say, pausing to take a long sip of my drink. "I had an idea for a sculpture series... that day, before I went out to meet you on Tompkins

Avenue. I haven't felt like doing more drawing of what I want to do yet, but I need space, a lot more space than I have in my apartment, and I can't afford rent for both. And I sure can't afford a model..."

"I'll model for you," Freddie says. "In exchange for coffee."

"It's not all that easy. I speak from experience."

"Okay, so coffee and an occasional lunch. I want to see what you've got going there. And I can talk to Mustafa about a place where you can work. I think his father owns a couple of warehouses. He might have some space that won't cost an arm and a leg."

"That...would be fantastic," I say, thinking of the hurried sketches I did that day and what I could do with them, what I'll now have a chance to do with them.

"What do you say we drink to it?"

"Yes," I say, raising my sweating glass. "To 'Gurl Power.' "

ACKNOWLEDGEMENTS

I'd like to thank members of the NYPD for their gracious cooperation and generous assistance (without which I would have felt even more like a rookie describing their world), as well as members of the Yale Police Department. Special mention goes to members of the Writers' Rendezvous in Westport for their encouragement and support, so appreciated especially as I finished writing this novel.

Thank you to my editor and publisher Lou Aronica for his vision and suggestions.

Thank you to my family, Bob, Meri, Michael and David, who always have my back, and to my friends who believed in me and this book and kept propelling me forward.

And thank you to Max and Kingston for your never-ending love and devotion.

ABOUT THE AUTHOR

Susan Israel lives in Connecticut with her beloved dog, but New York City lives in her heart and mind. Her first novel, *Over My Live Body*, was published by The Story Plant in 2014. A graduate of Yale College, her fiction has been published in *Other Voices*, *Hawaii Review* and *Vignette*, and she has written for magazines, websites and newspapers, including *Glamour*, *Girls Life*, *Ladies Home Journal* and *The Washington Post*. She's currently at work on the third book in the Delilah Price series.